Odyssey Down Under

Canadian Adventure
From the Tropics
to the
Far Northland

JAMES GARDNER

NEWMAN SPRINGS PUBLISHING
320 Broad Street
Red Bank, NJ 07701

First originally published by Newman Springs Publishing 2024

ISBN 979-8-89061-472-8 (Paperback)
ISBN 979-8-89061-473-5 (Digital)

Printed in the United States of America

It was Samoa, a fantastic tropical afternoon. Leilani and I had just been home a little while from what she called church. She is always pretty persuasive to goad me into going. But it's a good thing! The Samoan folks believe that they have always been here. They believe this was once the Garden of Eden and the Great Creator placed them here, really! If you ask where they came from, they look at you puzzled and say, "From here."

But it was a good day of song and dancing and good talks—all coming down from the missionaries who came to the islands after Captain James Cook had charted and explored these South Pacific Islands.

Leilani and I were ready to slow down, gear down, and lie down. We were ready to kick back and enjoy the day. Always on a Sunday afternoon, if the phone tinked, I knew who it would be!

I picked up a familiar chuckle on the other end, "Hello, James, how is it going?"

The Odyssey Down Under, which started in the first book, had blossomed into a continuing story. Book one was the first story that was the meeting of Captain Mobley. The book then became a double book in which James travels with Captain Mobley to the South Sea Islands, their tropical beauty, and their stories. That book then became a double book where Captain Mobley and James set a course into the North Pacific—destination, the Aleutian Islands. Many ports going north were visited in the course of the journey. In *Return to Fiji,* the saga continues with an introduction to Hawk, an Ojibwa Indian from Canada and how he becomes Curt's partner. Through this mix, we were on a flight to Fiji to meet Hawk's Uncle Magnus McGregor. Magnus took us on a Fiji Island tour and introduced us to Blight Waters. So come aboard with us to explore more of the North and South Pacific Islands and the stories we have to tell. As we traveled, Captain Mobley was anxious to take us to more places that will come up in the future.

"Well, that remains to be seen, Captain. What's on your mind?"

"Well, James, is it too early for another journey, and would you come be my first mate?" I looked back at Lei with a frown on her face, and I shook my head yes. The instant she knew Captain Mobley was on the line, her spirits fell. Not in a bad way though! She just hates to be without me, and that is a good thing!

"Well, James, no plan yet, but this is what it is about. Do you remember when we went to Fiji with Hawk? Remember, it's the homecoming he was all excited about, you knowing his mentor, Eagle Feather? And saying that sometime you and him should return there and have a time with Eagle Feather?" The questions were coming hard and fast. Somehow I thought this was going to be "mission impossible."

"Wow, Cap.," I said, "let's ease into this. Are you talking about Mountain Ash Lake in Canada?"

"Yes, James, where you had an encounter with a white wolf pup!" That comment got me right in the gut, and I started to tear up. Lei came to me and held on!

In a moment I said, "Sorry, Captain, that was a long time ago and deep in my heart!"

Captain said, "I'm sorry, James, I didn't mean it wrong."

"I'm okay now, Cap. Give me some background. Gosh, that is two worlds away."

He let out a soft chuckle. "Well, James, Hawk has been twisting my arm. I didn't say yes, but we have been going over maps. He wants to fly. I want to sail! His way would be to fly over and meet us at Vancouver Island, North Pacific, and fly us in. By sea, I would have to take the canal again, go up the Coast of America to Canada, where the Saint Lawrence Bay and River wait inland, down past Quebec and Montreal, then follow through the Great Lakes and make our way to St. Joseph Island again, where I met you, and then Hawk flies us up to Mountain Ash Lake!" he said all in one breath and sounded winded.

"I said, either way is a nice journey but does not make sense."

"That's what I told Hawk." He calmed down a bit. "I told Hawk this was a no-no" unless he could come up with a better plan! And you know, the bugger did!" He went on, "Hawk called his old employees at Land and Forest. They made some contacts and set it up for him. Also, they were anxious to see their favorite buddy! They contacted the forestry, and here is what they set up. We just have to give them time and dates or comply with their schedule. The forestry at Vancouver Island will check Hawk and passengers in and give clearance. Also, they will have a De Havilland Beaver fueled and ready. Hawk will then be required to fly passengers and crew to Thunder Bay for a stop, fuel, and check-in, then free to go wherever! Something in reverse on the return. James, you couldn't trade a gold mine for that!" I was speechless.

I asked, "How is Hawk going to contact Eagle Feather in the North Woods?"

"I asked him that, James, and he said Eagle Feather already knows and is looking forward to spending time with his old friend."

Then I asked Hawk, "How did you contact him?"

And all Hawk would say was, "We Indians have our ways! So, James, here sits the golden opportunity for us, pending your agreement. I need my first mate!"

"Oh brother, now what do I do?" I paused and said to Captain Mobley, "I won't go unless Leilani goes with me!"

Captain roared with laughter! "That's a good go, mate. She's onboard!"

I was stunned. "Wait a minute, Captain, how is the crew going to take this?"

"First of all, James, I'm captain. What I say goes! But think about this: we have had all the girls onboard, even Sheila, for trips back from Samoa. Also I took some diversions for them on these trips. Everybody's good!"

Then I said, "What about Sheila?"

Captain replied, "I ran this whole Hawk thing by her. I asked if she would go. She said, 'Lovely, go, Dick, but really I need to be here with young Dick and run this cattle station. Another time and we will. How do you think James will respond when you ask? And you know he and Leilani are thick!' I told her I was sure that would come up and I'd handle it softly Then she said, 'Dick, when did you ever handle anything soft?'"

Then he roared again with laughter, which was music in my ears. Old Captain Mobley was back to his old self! I said, "So it's a deal, Captain. Give me a time and a date. I think it's a good deal for a sea trip with both the crew and the flyers!" I hung up and looked at Leilani, tapping her foot.

She says, "What kind of mess have you got me into this time, Ollie?"

I said, "Wait a minute, that's my line."

She laughed and came into my arms. "I love you, James, and I will go to the ends of the earth with you, if you want!"

I didn't speak, but my mind was reeling. How did I ever get gifted with an angel like this?

"So," she says, "where are we going?"

I said, "Over the equator into the North Pacific, a stop at Hawaii, then North to Vancouver Island. There we will leave the ship. Everyone boards an aircraft like Hawk's and flies to the Northwoods, landing at a little place called Mountain Ash Lake, the most beautiful place I've seen in my travels, with the exception of here. There I will introduce you to an old friend I know named Eagle Feather, who is a great man to his tribal people!"

Leilani says, "Wow, James, I guess I am excited, like a big honeymoon. I've never been North. It will be exciting to see your old haunts, as you call them. The trip to your home place to get Cocoa was a real experience! Also, what about Cocoa?"

"Well, Cocoa's been with Curt and another friend whom Cocoa has taken to, so it will be okay until we get back. Curt's friend will stay here at our place until we return."

Another big hug! "Well, Lei, let's kick back and enjoy our time together until the ship comes in!'"

And the day the ship was coming in, Leilani and I were sitting on the dock of the bay, watching the *Sheila* approach from the horizon. What a beautiful sight. It would be a little while for the ship to make harbor. My thoughts went to Lei. Being a flight attendant on Qantas Air, she had crossed the equator on every trip from Australia to L.A., so nothing new there. Also, on many flights, they encountered turbulence, along with zipping in and out of time zones. She was looking at me in deep thought and asked, "James, what are you thinking about?"

"Well, sweetie, I was thinking about you and your travels across the equator, time zones, and such. Time zones slip by, and you don't know whether you are in day or night. It seems like there is no day! Only sixteen grinding hours of cramped travel. So—this journey will be different at sea. You will have to learn to get your sea legs, for one thing. You will be traveling much slower, and you will experience each day as it goes. You will go from the tropics to a cooler, or even colder, climate once we reach Vancouver, so I'm hoping for a smooth sail!"

She looked at me and said, "James! I have been in a canoe!"

I laughed but I said, "Turbulence in the sea?"

"Yes," she said, "and very rough seas at that." She sat, thinking about what I said, then asked, "James, will sea turbulence be as severe as air turbulence?"

I chuckled and said, "You betcha! But you just hang on to me, and we will make it through!" Then I chuckled while I watched the expression on her face. "Lei, chances are we will have a good trip, barring the unexpected. But we have a good captain and a good ship, so we will handle anything that comes up. I just wanted to inform you that sea travel can have its bad times, although with the time of year and the fine weather, it will be a good go!"

The ship was about to "kiss" the dock. So we holstered our gear, which was a sleeping bag each, a travel pouch for Lei, and a ditty bag for me. I traveled with this old canvas bag since navy years. We had put some extra clothing inside the sleeping bags just in case; Captain Mobley had a good supply of foul-weather gear onboard if needed.

Captain greeted us coming off the gangway with a grin, hand-shake, and "Welcome aboard, you two! I see you have your 'swags'" Swags is the Aussie term for sleeping bag). Then he chuckled. "I thought I could catch you two sleeping in." He laughed with a twinkle in his eye. "All secure, James?"

"Aye, Cap., all secure."

Onboard, Captain took the wheel and guided us out of the Samoan Harbor. Then we swung around the island to the east and headed north. Lei was struck with the wind, the sails, and the feel of the deck. When we were on course, he stepped in and took the wheel, taking the first watch. Captain said, "Step over here, Lei, and Mr. Helman will show you the controls and what they do." All wide-eyed, she stepped over. Captain said, "If fair weather prevails, we should make Hawaii in a few days. First stop will be Kealakekua Bay. hat is the site where our notorious Captain James Cook met his doom." "I want to see that bronze plaque again. You know, Lei, your love, James, gave us a spellbinding story on the life and journey of Captain Cook!"

Lei said, "Yes, I know. I've started to read!" Captain smiled. Next, the crew all lined up, tipping their hats and introducing themselves to Lei. Cookie was last; as usual, he had his little quip!

"Stick with me on this journey, Leilani, and you will come back a gourmet cook!" Everybody laughed at that one. Then Curt and Hawk stepped forward, hugging us both. They were old friends to us now, so all introductions complete, everyone returned to their duties. That left Curt, Hawk, Captain Mobley, Lei, and me to have some chitchat time and maybe a story or two. Later, everyone went their own way. I then took Lei to our lovely cabin for a rest.

I asked, "Comfortable, Lei?"

She said, "Yes, this is fantastic, and I feel safe and comfortable with the crew." Then she added, "When you have to take the watch, James, I want to stand with you."

I said, "That will be great, honey, but not required. You will enjoy that peacefulness, and Captain and I will hang together. You can get firsthand accounts of our stories."

As we moved north, some islands came into view. Lei and I were standing at the wheel with Captain Mobley. He grinned. "Look at that sight. Just think, Captain Cook saw this as he was heading north. He did not realize there were more islands above the equator." Yes, the sight at a distance was a beautiful panorama of South Sea Islands with the mountains and the tropical vegetation. But as we drew close, civilization started to appear—roads, houses, hotels on the beach, cars on the highway. Nobody said much. Captain had Kealakekua Bay right on course. As we moved into the bay, the real world came into view with all its structures—highway running close to the beach edge and A Pizza Hut and hot dog stand just across the road.

I said to Captain, "Welcome to the US of A!" Nonetheless, we were where Captain James Cook took his last stand and died while a thousand nations put him under attack. On this third voyage, he wanted to perform for his country, and he did, but death he did not expect in that service. Yet always there was that threat.

Captain had the *Sheila II* anchored, and boats were lowered to take us to shore. Once ashore, we found where the memorial plaque lay there on the Pacific shore. We also found some warm coals from a fire some campers had left nearby. With some firewood left. Hawk stoked up the coals, and soon we had a nice fire going. We saw one of the crew across the road for Dog n Suds. We all gathered around the fire and ate our dogs.

Then Cookie said, "Best damn dog I ever had!" Everybody roared with laughter.

Then I said, "Well, folks, this is as good as it gets!" and laughter broke out again. But we were not here for a picnic. We were here to, shall I say, honor our hero, Captain James Cook. And this was what we did. As the sun began to slip down into the horizon, it cast a reddish, golden glow over the memorial plaque, which was submerged under a few feet of water. We gathered together, quiet and solemn, as the waves gently moved to and fro around the plaque. With the sun and water movement, it shimmered and looked almost alive. We all saluted to the memory of the good captain, the excellent man.

Captain Mobley then said, "God bless you, Captain James Cook. May your soul rest in peace in the beloved Pacific that you loved so well." After a moment of silence, satisfied, we returned to the boats and boarded the ship. And as we made preparations to retire to our quarters, Captain asked, "James, will you be our tour guide on these islands?"

I said, "Sure will, Cap."

"So what stop should be next, mate?"

I replied, "The main island is a busy place, and I'm not sure it's a good go for the crew. Let's head next, down to, or should I say, north to Maui. Tour there, then strike out north for Vancouver Island."

"Sounds like a good plan to me, mate!"

Bright and early the next morning, we weighed anchor and headed for Maui. Arriving at Maui Harbor, we found a good portage where we could tie off the ship and lay down the gangway. I went alone on shore. There was a travel agency conveniently there to serve incoming guests. I requested a bus or two vans to travel together for a tour. I said it would be twelve people. I wanted to specify where I wanted to go and not take a guided tour. The man looked at me a little strange, shrugged his shoulders, and said, "Okay, sir, I have just what you want: two vans and two 'Kanaka' boys to drive." *Kanaka'* is a term used for islanders.

When the vans pulled up to the ship, one driver waved the other off. He said, "Don't need you. I have room comfortable for twelve. I will reimburse this gentleman!" I thanked the boy for that, and he gave me a big pearly white grin in return. He looked at the ship tied off, as did many other spectators in the area.

"Wow!" he said. "You're no Captain Cook, are you?"

I laughed. "No, son, that was long, long ago. Now if you want to meet a real captain, Captain Mobley, commander of this ship, will be coming along." The pearly white grin persisted. As the group disembarked from the ship, introductions were made all around. When it came to Leilani, his eyes widened.

"Wow," he exclaimed, "she is beautiful! Is she Hawaiian?"

I replied, "Sorry, no, she's Samoan and also my wife!"

Again, he said, "Wow. You're a lucky man!" We all laughed.

Then he asked, "Where to?"

I recounted where we wanted to go and see. "We'll go to the blowhole, then see the black sands, then to the volcano, then dive through the city, with stops anywhere anyone wants. Then I want the best gourmet meal in Maui!"

So he said, "I'll take you to the best on the island. It's Japanese-owned: a fabulous restaurant, gardens, all open air, condos all around, and a buffet table. You must have the buffet table because it has everything! It will pop your eye. Any kind of food you desire will be on the buffet. For little money, you can try a little of everything. Don't pass up the pineapple. It's picked at the peak of ripeness and is heavenly!" All this was said with a perpetual grin.

I responded, "Good show," and we loaded up and were off. He was the driver and also acted as our tour guide, giving explanations at all stops. The first stop was the blowhole—a tourist must—a huge hole in the coral reef. As the sea surged in, a gigantic waterspout roared up out of the hole over and over. When we got there, Leilani had never experienced a blowhole. When the first big blow came up from the hole, which is quite huge, she screamed and clutched onto me. I didn't mind.

I said, "Hang on, honey. Another one's coming." The whole group was truly fascinated. You didn't want to walk away; you wanted to wait for the next blow. I remarked that we were off the island right now, standing on a coral reef. Examining the coral, many species of sea life and vegetation could be seen preserved in the coral itself. If you find an open space away from the sea breakers, you may see tropical fish. We spent time there and enjoyed it to the fullest.

As we were loading up, Captain Mobley remarked, "Just this right here would have been worth the stop."

The driver announced, "Folks, I've brought box lunches and drinks. They're in the rear. Enjoy while we head to the black sands." It was a scenic drive. The smaller islands aren't as developed as the main island. We pulled into a small parking area, and in front of us was the beach—total black sand, no white.

I asked the driver, "Will you please tell me your name? You know all of ours by heart. I'm amazed. I don't want to say, 'Hey, driver,' when I want to address you!"

With a big grin, he replied, "You may not believe this, so hang loose, man! My name is Don Ho. I was named after the famous island singer. Remember? He sang like your Dean Martin."

I responded, "Yes, I remember that, and I'll call you Don, like my brother."

And Don Ho said, "You are my brother, man!" I was growing fond of this kid! Don Ho then said, "There's nothing here that's exciting or spectacular, but what I love is that it's the most primitive place on the island. Walk around a bit and take it in. I'll wait." And spectacular it was: total black sand and not a soul on the beach. Not a footprint in the sand. Coconut palms swayed in the wind above the sand. We all took a walk down the beach, and, on our way back looked at our footprints in the black sand—the only footprints. I remarked, "Now, folks, you can say you left your footprint in the black sands of Maui." We sat under the coconut palms in the tropical breeze, gentle and fresh. I could imagine, in my mind's eye, an old three-masted ship trying to carefully make it to shore, maybe through coal, maybe coming ashore in a longboat: the first explorers to set foot on this beach. After a while, we were ready to leave. We returned to the van, and I directed, "To the volcano, Don Ho!" And away we went, arriving at the volcano site, which was a long climb for the van up the mountain.

Don announced, "The guide here will show you the crater. I'll wait."

I looked at him and quipped, "Okay, pal, but don't you move this van if you hear any rumbles."

He laughed heartily. "Okay, bro, I would never leave you guys!"

The guide came out to take us to the edge of the crater. He didn't say much—because what can you say about a massive hole in a mountain? He cautioned us to stay behind the rope and grinned. I sensed this guy was up to some mischief. He shared the history of the volcano, including past eruptions, lava flows, and more. Then he asked us to get as close to the rope as possible. We did, leaning over the rope to look way down—and I mean way down—into the crater. He explained that the volcano was dormant and hadn't erupted in years. Then pointing at a muddy substance at the bottom, he described it as a hot spring that bubbled constantly, pushing up mud and emitting steam. Offering a closer look, he jested he could lower us down on a rope. There were no takers.

He went on, "It's been a quiet old girl for eons—no rumble, no red lava, no belching steam." And with that, he playfully whacked his walking stick on the rope. I wasn't the only one startled. I think I was number one in line!

He chuckled. "You are a perfect group. I've enjoyed showing you the ins and outs." As we returned to the van, Don Ho was trying to hide his smirk.

The next part of our adventure was a tour of the town, which proved interesting. I was relieved that everyone was getting tired and we didn't need to visit the shops. That would come later on the return trip. True to his word, Don Ho pulled up to the entrance of the most beautiful hotel and condo we had ever seen. A pretty Japanese young girl escorted us into the dining area where everything was set up.

Don said, "I wait."

I said, "No, you will join our crowd. The bill is covered." He was so elated as he came in. The meal was everything he said and more. As good as a first class meal, Don Ho returned us to the ship.

As we departed, he said to Captain Mobley, "Captain Sid, has James taken you to Pearl Harbor and the Arizionia Memorial?"

"No," said the captain.

Then Don said, "It's a little out of the way to backtrack, but it is a must-see!" I tried to bring this to Captain's attention, and I regretted it. Captain sensed that.

He said, "Well, Don Ho. Good point. Said we'll make that a go before we leave these islands." Then he shook hands goodbye with Don.

We boarded the ship. A good night's sleep was in store; everyone was happy and satisfied. "Folks, we get underway in the morning bright and early. James will show us Pearl Harbor on the main island. After that, James will tell us what's next before he turns us loose!"

Hawk was deep in thought. Then he asked James, "Are all these people Hawaiians?"

I said, "Yes, they are all Hawaiian citizens, which they choose to be but also intertwined with many different cultures—English, Scots, Chinese, Japanese, Portuguese, etc." He pondered on it for a moment. Then he said, "If I were to make a choice to stay here, I could introduce Indian!"

Everyone laughed. Captain Mobley then said, "Look, Hawk, Captain Cook would not allow his men to jump ship and stay in the islands. Neither is it going to happen here, mate!" Everyone roared with laughter, then off to bed for a good night's sleep.

In the morning, we got underway and set our course south for Pearl Harbor. We were reversing our course back to the big island, but after seeing Pearl, we would again head up through the North Pacific. As we approached Pearl Harbor, I said to the captain., "We don't need to make a stop here. When we get to the Arizona Memorial, please circumvent the structure." I also asked the crew if they would indulge me and put on their old-fashioned uniforms that were prevalent of the original HMS *Vanguard*. They were glad and excited to do that. We moved into the harbor and set our sights on the position of the memorial. As we came abreast, the captain slacked sails a bit and began his circle.

He handed the wheel over to the helm and said, "Slow circle around, mate! Then head out to the Pacific Ocean again."

"Aye, sir," said Helm, taking the wheel. That also put him in a good position for viewing. The crew lined up at the rail in their uniforms, with the rest of the passengers plus Captain Mobley. Helm approached the site on our starboard side and began a slow, easy circle around.

I said, "Folks, as we pass around this memorial, the USS *Arizona*, sunk with most of its crew still onboard, down to a watery grave. They served their country with honor until downed by the Japanese torpedo bombers. May those boys rest in peace!" When we were abreast of the port side of the memorial, the crew stood at attention in their uniforms and gave a firm salute, which was held until we were past. All of us saluted, even Helm at the wheel. Captain had on his military commander's hat.

The ship eased by in full sail with the American flag and Australian flag flapping on the pinnacle. Tears came to my eyes. It was too moving. I wondered how many visitors, plus naval crew, were attending the *Arizona* that day. If so, they sure did get an extra treat!

Captain nodded to Helm, and Helm understood and stayed on the wheel. We were heading back to sea. As we broke out of the bay into open sea, Captain looked at me and said, "James, there's more story to this. Why don't you tell us about it?"

"Okay," I said, "when the ship was hit and in flames, sinking into the bay, the call for abandon ship was called. Boats were lowered, sailors jumping into the water with life jackets. The ones below deck were trapped and would go down with the ship. There were six men trapped on a gun mount. Water all around, a boatswain was standing on deck across from them, thinking how he could get them off. His division officer ran back before he got off the ship and yelled at him, 'Get off the ship now, sailor, that's an order!' The sailor looked at him and refused, shook his head no. He was a tough old bugger anyhow. Rough around the edges, a scrapper at times, and just didn't give a damn. He hustled below and came back with a heaving line, monkey fist attached. He heaved the line to the gun mount. The sailor secured the line and one by one came across. The boatswain mate pulled them to safety one by one. They all survived that day, and to my knowledge, four or five of the six were still alive. They flew to Hawaii and attended an honorable service on the sunken ship memorial in honor of his name."

We were quiet for a while, and Leilani said, "Not to be disrespectful, James, but what is a monkey fist?"

We all laughed. Then Captain Mobley offered the answer for me. "Lei, a monkey fist is a lead ball woven into a hand line, like the ones we have onboard. It's used to throw out and measure the depth of the water when you are traveling in shallows to keep you out of harm's way. Captain most likely used his depth finder many times."

"Now I understand," said Lei, then looking at me, she said, "James, did you ever use a monkey fist?" Captain chuckled as he looked at me.

"I knew there was going to be a good story time on this trip!"

I laughed with him and said, "Yes, Capt., I'm afraid many will be told."

Captain smiled and said, "The more the better."

We were now moving deep into the Pacific. I turned back to Lei. "No, Lei, I never used a monkey fist, but I watched one used when I was transferred to the First 880. We were en route across the Atlantic. To back up a bit, I went aboard with another crew I did not know. When I was shown the living compartment, there was a mate lying in his bunk. He turned and said, 'Hey!' I had gone through basic with him, a good buddy. I expressed my joy and said I had at least one friend onboard, 'But not for long, pal. I have a bad appendix, and they are going to transfer me onto a hospital ship.' That made me sad to lose my buddy so quickly. Being at sea, I pondered how a transfer was going to be made. That answer came two days later when we saw a navy destroyer bearing down on our port side. A seaman threw a monkey fist over to the deck of the destroyer. They attached a bigger line, and we drew it across. Then an even bigger line to that, which we drew across, one that would carry weight. Calhoun was all bundled up because it was cold. Then a bosun chair was attached to the rope line, and Calhoun was placed in it with safety straps. The heavy line was then attached to our winch and also to theirs. The winches started, one undoing and the destroyer's winch taking up. Just about the middle of the transfer, somebody misjudged, and poor ole Calhoun was dipped into the sea. We all yelled in anger! He was popped right back up, soaked, and looking like a drowned rat! But he raised his arm in triumph! He was now on the destroyer to be transferred to a hospital ship. I was glad that ole Calhoun would receive treatment and recover, but I was sad because I knew that I would never see him again. So, Lei, that's my experience with the monkey fist." Lei was in awe.

Captain said, "James, there is more to that journey, and I will twist your arm later to finish that story!"

So farther up the North Pacific, the ship plied; our next port of call would be Vancouver. Hawk and Curt were in the background listening as I turned. They grinned and said, "James, we are not going to miss any stories!" We all had a good laugh. As we went on, day by day, the weather was good—clear sky and gentle seas. I was glad for Lei.

One night, or I should say early evening (because we still had a good sun and a calm sea), Captain called the crew together. With Helm at the wheel, we could see him gather close for all to hear. It was like the time we gathered together to tell the stories about Captain Bligh and Captain Cook, only this time we were still at sea, not sitting around an island campfire. Captain said, "James, it's time to hear the rest of the story about one of your Atlantic Sea trips. I have taken the liberty to tell the crew about your monkey fist story. We may be in the Pacific, but this time we are going to talk about the Atlantic!"

A little embarrassed, but I like to tell stories, I had Lei sit close to me before I began. "Well, the First 880 was deployed for this journey to take a battalion of sea bees down to Cuba, Guantanamo Bay, for a construction job down there. Then we were to go back up to Rhode Island and be loaded with eight hundred pounds of steel panels, then out to sea. That's where the monkey fist story comes in—to cross the Atlantic to Morocco, located on the North Morocco eastern coast of Africa, very close to the Mediterranean Sea. After a long sea journey of sixteen days, I had seen seas with twenty-foot swells that could capsize us to one day of complete calm where the sea met the sun on the horizon like a piece of glass. So spectacular that it was hard to leave sight of it and go for duty calls! There was a port where we were going and also a river feeding into the waters of the port. We did not stop at the port! An Arab river pilot was put onboard and took the helm to guide us up the river channel. "No monkey fists were used!"

Everyone laughed. "The crew was a little nervous about an Arab taking the captain's place. Let me say here, we did not have a full captain, per se, but the executive officer was assigned duties of his own, plus filling in for the captain. He probably got command of the ship later, but I never knew. Anyhow, up the river, we were not told the reason for the steel or trip, and we would not be told! The steel was going to a small base, then just outside of Medina. The base was open to the river. We pulled close to their pier and tied off. No steel was yet to be unloaded. I looked at the corrugated steel and thought, this isn't pier decking. It almost looks like a barrier wall. Then a marine officer came over and got into a chat with us. 'Boy, are we ever glad to see you guys pull in. We just about got into a bad way with the Arabs. Seems like the French had exiled one of their great leaders. The Arab government, such as it is, demanded his return! The French refused! The Arabs put out a decree—partner with the US or we will attack, not only you, but we will wipe out the Americans on the base! That is our soil! So just before you pulled in, there must have been an agreement. For three days, a thousand mounted tribesmen sat on their horses with Khyber rifles. They sat silent from dawn to dark. At night we would see campfires, and at dawn, they were back. The ultimatum was three days. This is day four, and they must have gotten their leader back because the shoreline was deserted! Pal, if they had crossed the river, we would have been wiped out! We only have a fifty-caliber machine gun and our small arms. If it came, we were done. If it did say you were here, those guns on the ship and the crew armed would have been on equalizer! It was quite a relief, and we were thankful.' I looked as the steel was being unloaded, and I thought, *Huh, looks like a steel barrier to me, to be built on the riverside.*

"We stayed there for four days before getting clearance to return. Day one, all liberty ashore denied. Day two, liberty for part of the crew. I lucked out. A buddy and I went to the bazaar or open market. It was the buddy system, not to go alone because conditions were still likely to erupt. Once in, it was amazing to see all the shops and wares. We were told not to exchange our US dollars there. Go to a bank. Well, there was no bank! I learned later that the shopkeepers could take the US dollars and sell at a profit to the Russian government. As we walked around, a young man, Arabic, approached me. He was dark-skinned, handsome, with coal-black hair, neatly groomed, in a white shirt, black pants, and expensive European shoes. He walked up to me, greeted me, and gave his name. He asked if I would like to have my money changed. I said, 'If I do, are you going to fly away with my money, never to be seen again?' He said, 'No, no, no, I will return.' So I took out what I wanted changed and said, 'I'm going to trust you!' He said, 'You can trust me!' The exchange went smoothly and quickly, and I had French Francs to spend. I took fifty Francs (which did not valuate high) and handed them to the young man. He said he did not expect that. I said, 'I want you to have this because I trusted you, and you came through for me!' We shook hands, and he disappeared into the crowd. The next evening, with the other half of the crew on liberty, the duty officer came to me and said, 'We will have you picked up and taken to the town police station. You are our assistant man to help the base sailor with shore patrol (military police).' The police station obviously was French. I was greeted by three navy personnel from the base. One would be my partner, or rather "his" partner, and the other two would man the jeep and transport us.

"The police officer handed us a watch belt and a light stick. My partner asked, 'Where's my forty-five?' The policeman said, 'No guns, use the stick. We are to show a sign of peace!' My partner said, 'Yeah, with my hide!' The two jeep drivers laughed. We loaded up in the jeep and left town. 'What's our duty?' I asked. 'Outskirts of Medina, women's prison,' they said. 'Not to worry, we will come through every half hour to check on you.' When we got there and were put out, the instruction was, 'Stay by that brick wall. Do not wander into the courtyard unless you see someone approach the prison! No matter uniform or civilian clothes, if US military, turn them away!' Well, so much for that! So standing against the brick wall, I asked my partner what the woman's prison was all about. He said that the women were locked up. They were required to give favors to men to pay their fine. But I didn't know of anybody ever getting out.

"So we had four hours to stand guard and check for jeeps every half hour. We stood and watched, and the courtyard watched also! Time slipped by—no jeep! We would feel the tension increasing! My partner said, 'If any of these cooks approach, don't talk! Use your stick! Go for the head and throat, nobody, that won't stop them!'

"That sure was a comfort talk for a little swabby in a foreign environment. Just about when things might escalate, the handsome young money changer strolled into the courtyard. He approached me and asked, 'How are you?' We had a brief conversation, then he half turned and looked at the people in the courtyard. He said, 'Shake my hand.' So I did. While he grasp my hand, he called out to the Arabs. 'This is my friend!' Still shaking my hand, he continued, 'If any of you decide to bring harm to my friend You will have to deal with me!' Then he turned to me and said, 'You are my friend, and no one will dare approach you in anyway. I must go now, but it has been a pleasure to serve you!' And he walked off into the darkness, never to be seen again!

"My partner turned to me and said, 'Wow! Man, how did you meet him?' I said, 'Well, it's a long story!' A short while later, the jeep pulled up, and my partner jumped them. 'Well, we got our four hours in, but where the heck were you guys?' 'You have any trouble?' they asked. Partner said, 'No! But we might have succeeded, if it wasn't for those guys.' So the next day, our mission was completed, and we pulled out! This time our ex-officer was allowed to depart up the river. I guess I could say that the sixteen days back across, the Atlantic did not look too bad!"

There was complete silence! All eyes on me made me nervous, so I said, "A side note to the story: after seven days at sea going to Morocco, we ran out of meat, milk, and bread. It was a bit unpleasant for the rest of the journey. We took on supplies, and on the return trip, we had all the milk we could drink. The meat was plentiful, and the bread was something fresh baked there. It was shaped like a little football with a hard glazed crust and a soft center. It was so delicious that I've never had anything like it since, but I can taste it in my memory."

Then ole Cookie piped up, "No shortage on this cruise, James! I will see to that!" Laughter all around. Leilani was hanging on me, wide-eyed and tight. I loved every moment of that.

In due time, thanks to the captain's expert course calculations, Vancouver Island was on the horizon. As we moved closer, we could see breakers lapping on the rough shoreline; the tall pines looked spectacular as we approached. Captain Mobley made a slight turn to the south to approach the opening at South Point, where the inlet lay between the island and the mainland. There wouldn't be any reef here to contend with! We moved north through the inlet, passing cottages and businesses. When Hawk spotted the Beaver, a Dehavilland, resting and moored to a dock, the captain edged us in and found ample room for our docking. We secured the ship good and tight. She would be resting here for a while.

Security approached us and was a happy old captain. After shaking hands all around, he suggested that our ship would be just fine and safe until our return. It seemed like he knew all about our venture. He pointed to the immigration check-in and mentioned that the forestry division was just north of it. When we went into immigration, they were all smiles. "You folks are already cleared to go, but we just need a headcount and origin."

I spoke up, "We have a captain, eight seamen all from Australia, one lovely Samoan lady, two flyers both from Samoa, and me from the United States."

The lady responded, "The people from Samoa, American Samoa, right?"

"Yes," I replied.

"Then they are American citizens." She made a note of that. I looked at Hawk and grinned. He was no longer an "Indian" from Canada but a US citizen.

As we walked out, a jeep loaded up front. Two burly guys with beards, grinning from ear to ear, said, "Welcome! We are the Forestry Bots! Ontario worked through us to get you folks onboard! We are instructed to give 'Hawk' a big hug, in case he can't get down to see the old gang!" They grabbed Hawk and lifted him off the ground between them in a big bear hug, laughing. We all had to join in.

Then they said, "Hawk, there's your Beaver, ready to go! Extra fuel aboard. You will be required to land at Thunder Bay for a check-in and flight plan for destination in Ontario! You're good to go, son. Happy landings!"

We retrieved all our gear and supplies off the *Sheila II* and stowed them away in the Beaver. All aboard, and Hawk slid open the side window and yelled, "Clear!" Then he started the engine. We moved away from the dock, and Hawk pushed the throttle forward. We were skimming down the inlet, then liftoff—airborne! Hawk banked toward the inland, and soon we were flying high over the great pines of Canada. We were all excited about our destination. Flying was surely faster than sea travel. In what seemed like no time, Thunder Bay on Lake Superior came into view. After touchdown, Hawk spoke to the tower.

They replied, "No need to get out, Hawk. We will send out a rep. Just need a headcount and flight plan for your destination. I understand it's Mountain Ash Lake?"

"Yes," said Hawk. "Okay, buddy, sign the paperwork and you're off."

Again, we were airborne. As we approached the lake area—a total forest and huge lake—I was astounded. I hadn't realized the lake was that large. Hawk circled the lake twice to give us all a look at where we would be. Then Hawk spotted the old pier, banked again for an approach, and we drifted down, landing on the water like a big Canadian goose. Exhilarating is all I can say! We taxied to the pier, where an old indigenous man was waiting, dressed in buckskin with a tomahawk on one hip and a bowie knife on the other. Two eagle feathers adorned his braided hair, clearly signifying who he was.

"Eagle Feather," Hawk quickly secured the plane and opened the access door for us. Then he turned and embraced the old man, tears in his eyes, speaking in Ojibwe. I was next, and I guess I was so happy to see him again, I did the same, though without speaking Ojibwe. We made introductions right then and there, and I had told the folks about Eagle Feather long before – about what his feathers meant and how he was held in high esteem by his tribe. He chose to live in this North Forest and its solitary life, with his wolf dog by his side. Our next job was unloading the gear, and Eagle Feather was right there helping.

Cookie asked, "What's the deal with the pier?"

Eagle Feather smiled and said, "That will be my story tonight around the campfire."

We all reached the campsite, and I was amazed. In all these years, the campsite hadn't changed. I remarked to Eagle Feather about this, and he simply said, "Sacred ground." I knew better than to question further, but it still pondered my mind. Wolf dog came over, sidled up to me, and I gave him a good petting. Eagle Feather remarked, "And Cocoa, whom you sometimes call Buck? This wasn't a journey for him, so he's with friends." Eagle Feather nodded in approval. He then called our attention.

"I will have you call me Eagle for short!" He looked at Leilani and said, "Young lady, I will call you Lei." I was amazed. How did he know that?

"Captain, I will address you as Captain. Next I will call you Helm because your hands tell me you guide the ship well! And I will call you Cookies because anyone that ask, what's this pier about can only be a cook!" Then he smiled and everyone had a good laugh.

"And you gentlemen at the crew, too many names to remember, so I will call you friend because you are now my friends." Now, Eagle Feather is too long to be always repeating, and my real name is Mackutuck." Well, so much for introductions—Eagle made things easy! He proceeded to put more wood on the fire.

Helm, curious as ever, asked, "Eagle, what kind of wood is this?"

Eagle replied, "I will explain this to you."

Return

of the

White Wolf

A story from the imagination

Front cover: Art by Juanita Honeycutt and design by Candace Johnson.

Return

of the

White Wolf

A story from the imagination

Acknowledgment

I wish to thank Juanita Honeycutt for her permission to use her artwork for the front cover and Candace Johnson for her assistance to bring this front cover to reality. All other photos are from my collection.

RETURN *of the* WHITE WOLF

JAMES A. GARDNER

Introduction

Many years ago, I spent nine consecutive years making a trip to Little Rapids, Canada, to spend time there with my friends Glen and Evie Brethour. We would then go on north to an area called Mountain Ash Lake. This area was a paradise, with a pristine lake and a surrounding deep forest.

To get into this area, you had to take an old logging road that hadn't been used for a long time. It was a rough trip in but well worth the effort. On one of the trips with Glen, I fell down a steep slope, injuring my leg so badly that I couldn't walk. I went into survival mode and made provisions to bed down until help could arrive. During the night, I had an encounter with a female wolf and her pups.

This story was published in my wife's book *Beyond the Black Gate* by Anita Sutherland Gardner. I'll use the story again for chapter 1, and the following story will pick up from there. This story will be a tribute to my wife, Anita, and to my friends Glen and Evie Brethour. It will be written with a mix of true facts and my imagination. The story will reflect my obsession with the white wolf pup, the trips Anita and I took, and the times I shared with my friends and our stories together.

One Snowy Night

It was nearing dusk, and the snow was starting to fall. It gently settled on the white pine boughs in the area where I was standing in the Canadian wilderness. A beautiful area of bluffs, white pine mixed with hardwoods, a moving stream—all within my sight. The scenery was exhilarating, and for a moment, I was lost in its magic! Then a twinge of pain brought me back to reality and my situation.

A short time before, I had become separated from my Canadian friend on our hunt. Adding to the problem of being lost, I also stumbled and fell down a slope, injuring my leg. I tried to travel a short distance when the pain shot me down. So here I sat, not only lost but injured! Realizing I was completely disoriented on direction and not able to travel, the only logical thing to do was to stay put and in the general area. Maybe my location could possibly be determined by my friend Glen.

As I was sitting and evaluating my situation, a small buck quietly emerged from the pines ahead of me, up from the stream bank. He was apparently coming to drink. I very carefully and quietly aimed and dropped the young buck. I was very reluctant to do so, but in this situation, I would need food and water. Making my way down to the stream the best I could, I began skinning the hide and taking the best cuts of meat. I packed the cuts carefully within the hide. I then slipped the remains into the moving stream to allow the carcass to float on downstream and away from my general area. I was not too fond of the notions of sharing the remains with any predator that might drop by.

Night was falling fast, and my leg pain was increasing. *Not much time,* I thought. Staggering, half-walking, half-crawling, I pulled the hide of meat up and away from the stream into a stand of white pines a short distance away. The cover of pines might be enough for tonight's protection. Darkness was fast approaching, so I built a campfire at the edge of the pines and cooked a supper of venison. This was topped off with a drink of water from the stream where I had filled my canteen.

I settled down under the pines in the nettles and prepared for a long winter's night. The snow was gently falling, and the fire flickered in the darkness. My sleep was fitful with alternate bouts of dreaming and awakening and being very cold. The dawn awoke with a fresh cover of snow, and the wind was starting to pick up. With the temperature dropping and no help within hearing distance, I figured the next step would be shelter. I spent most of the day stumbling around hacking small saplings and cutting pine boughs with my hunting knife to construct a suitable lean-to for cover. Once complete, I moved the hide of the meat inside and retrieved some pieces for an evening meal. I had gathered enough firewood and scraps for the construction of the lean-to to support a good fire. After eating, I settled down for another uneventful night. The wind was picking up more and more, creating a fine mist and swirling snow. It howled and moaned simultaneously through the pines, mocking Old Man Winter himself. The fire flickered in the night and gave some warmth but not enough, because I was very cold and very sleepy, drifting in and out at times.

Something stirred me. I saw movement in the shadows of the misting, blowing snow. Startled, I awoke from this half-sleep, only to find that maybe it was my imagination, the fire and the swirling snow perhaps playing tricks on me. I started to drift off to sleep again, only to awake with a start! There! There on the edge of the dark and mist, barely illuminated by the firelight, stood a beautiful she-wolf! Our eyes met! We stared at each other intently, for quite some time. She stared with a quizzical look but not one of aggression. I very slowly reached for my hunting knife, careful not to make any quick moves. I gently unwrapped the deer hide and cut a piece of venison. I slowly raised it into the air for her to gain a scent. Then I gently tossed the meat beyond the edges of the fire. She quickly recovered the morsel and disappeared into the darkness. I felt sad, so to speak, but somewhat relieved.

Sleep was coming to me again, and I was enjoying the memory of the moment. The she-wolf, silver-gray, with dark black running down her back. Those steel-gray eyes that could stare right through you! *What a magnificent animal,* I thought. Sleep again was taking its toll on me. I drifted off, only to be aroused again by movement. As I gazed into the misting snow, I realized that she was back. I half rose and looked. With her were five wolf pups, all marked like her except one. He was larger than the rest, so I figured it had to be a male. Looking closer, I saw that he was pure white!

Once again, I opened the hide and cut pieces of venison to throw to the edge of the fire. The she-wolf entered the perimeter and gently retrieved them one by one, taking each back and laying it before her pups. When each had been satisfied, her steel-gray stare again returned to me, and I knew she was ready for her portion. I cut her portion of venison and gently tossed it to the fire's edge. She gently ate it with dignity with her pups at her side. This time they did not offer to leave but stayed within the edge of the firelight. The wind was becoming more intense now, and the snow was swirling into a fierce white-out.

Again I became very cold and very sleepy. My leg was throbbing with cold settling into my bones. I finally drifted off. Sometime later I was brought awake by strange movement! I awoke in fear but seemed to return to calm. I felt warmth against my back and leg. As I looked over my shoulder, the she-wolf had entered the lean-to and lain down beside me against my back! As I looked down behind my bent knees, there lay the five pups huddled up against the back of my legs fast asleep. Only the white pup roused briefly to look me straight in my eyes. Then he fell back into slumber.

I looked back at the she-wolf again, and there seemed to be an understanding in our exchanges of eye contact. I settled back into sleep, warm and content.

I was awakened in the morning by a low and mournful howl. I looked over to an adjacent bluff, and the she-wolf with her pups was silhouetted against the morning sun that was starting to appear through the white pines. There she sat, majestic as ever, her five pups sitting in front of her. The white pup was sitting in the forefront. Without a sound, we exchanged stares for the longest time. Then she turned, and she and her pups disappeared into the hardwoods.

Saddened, I wondered what had disturbed her. Then a distant noise told me. It was Glen and some rescue workers coming to retrieve me. As we were preparing to leave, once again I heard that mournful howl. Looking up on the far ridge, there she was again, her nose to the air and five little pups looking around intently!

Not many words were exchanged that day on the way out. One part of me said thanks to the ones that came for me, but I had a big sadness in my heart for the ones who had cared for me through the night! As she turned with the pups and again slipped into the trees out of sight, I vowed to lay down the gun and never again take the life of one of God's creatures placed upon this earth in His nature for man to enjoy. And when the winter winds howl and the snow swirls my memory, my thoughts go back to that she-wolf and her pups. To this day, my heart has mixed emotions about whether to go back to the world or just stay a little while longer in that wondrous nature. Experiencing in my heart "that" which maybe no other man may have felt in his lifetime!

Last Trip Together

The last trip I went on for our Canadian get-together was a bitter-sweet affair—sweet in the sense that I could be with my friends but bitter because I learned that Glen had a serious heart problem I did not know about.

During the summer, he acquired an old Volkswagen, stripped it down, and rebuilt it into a dune buggy. He fashioned it into a trail runner for us—really for his heart condition—but he laughed it off and said, "This is so we can ride in style!" The truth was, Glen could not walk fifty feet without becoming completely exhausted.

One night toward the end of the week, he had a massive heart attack. All efforts to revive him failed. I told Evie that I was going to take him home. The first phone was twenty miles away. We broke camp, loaded up, and with me driving in front and Glen lying in the back bed, we headed out. Evie had to drive Glen's truck, loaded with the dune buggy towing behind. She said, "I don't think I can do this. I am not a good driver."

I responded, "Evie, you have got to do it! You have to, and I know you can!" When we got to the first phone, I stopped and instructed Evie to call home to the law enforcement, doctor, and their funeral director. I stayed on until all arrangements were made, Evie was settled in, and I attended the funeral. Then I headed for home. That ended my trip to Canada.

A few years later, I met and married Anita. She shared my stories and memories of Canada and later wrote them down for her book, *Beyond the Black Gate*. Many times my mind would drift back to those times and also to the encounter with the white wolf pup and wonder about that outcome.

Living and Learning

We had our share of everyday life and what it brought. Along with that, we had our first home built. We still had time for travel, and we took many memorable trips, both short and long. The memories of Canada, Glen, and the white wolf pup always came back to my mind. I thought I would never go back!

Anita would always prompt me to tell stories about my Canadian adventures. Then one day, she said she would like to go to Canada and see some of the places I had been. So the trip was planned, and we headed north. We stopped along the way to see many places that I had passed by on my trips up. We passed through Grayling, Michigan, and viewed the National Forest. We took a look at the Au Sable River and Old Lodge. Further up, we stopped at Fort Mackinac and took a boat over to see Mackinac Island. We stayed in a private home that rented out the upstairs on Loon Lake in Upper Michigan. We crossed the International Bridge into Sault Ste. Marie. We headed east through the Indian Reservation and stopped at St. Joe. I showed her the docks and then returned to the camp to eat at Lorne's restaurant. Their special was chips and gravy—that is, french fries with homemade chicken gravy on top. We backtracked to the "Soo" to find lodging.

The next day, we took a train ride that went north into the wilderness. There were no roads, and people who had cabins up there went by this train. At one stop, a man pulled his canoe out of a boxcar and proceeded to enter the lake and paddle to his cabin on the other side. At different stops, they dropped off a block of ice, a newspaper, and continued on. The train took this run every day until winter.

Then we went east again to Little Rapids. We went to the stream where I used to fish for kokanee salmon. We drove through the tree plantation to see rows and rows of greenhouses raising pine seedlings for later reforestation projects.

Next we went north out of Little Rapids to the North Country and Mountain Ash Lake Country where the very last petrol (gas) station was. The power lines ended way back, so the station used a big diesel generator to power it. At the station, there was a wolf dog with one blue eye and one brown. He was very friendly. I asked the attendant if it was his. He said, "No, that wolf dog lives ten miles over the mountain. He comes every day to hang out with me and buy treats." I petted the wolf dog, and all the memories of my encounter with the wolf pack came flooding back into my mind. Then that old nagging thought—I wondered whatever happened to him?

A little further north, I turned onto a gravel road that was extremely rough. It went through the forest a couple of miles and opened to a clearing. Here was Bridal Veil Falls. The water was coming over the top and thundering down. Spectacular! Back out and north again, and I found the old Logging Road into Mountain Ash Lake. It had overgrown somewhat. I told Anita that we could chance it, but we didn't know what we might encounter. Sometimes there is water across the road from the beavers damming up the stream flow. Anita said we better not chance it and risk getting into trouble. It was a wonderful trip, and everything she had seen was putting my stories into reality.

Back Home

Back home, daily living seemed to let time slip by so fast that it was unreal. The years brought the need to downsize, caregiving for Anita's mom. We moved to the Arkansas family farm and more building cleanup. Before you know it, twenty years had passed. But memories stood still. I lost Anita!

Two Old Dogs

Memories don't stop; they stay with you. Ten years ago, Cocoa came to my window out of nowhere. I don't know where he came from, and I never found out! I am just glad that he came. He was a comfort to Anita and me through the bad times. We have been through ten years of living now and have become very attached. I tell folks that two old dogs live here. I talk to him like a person, and he seems to understand what I am saying. Sometimes he knows my thoughts without me speaking them. In turn, watching his actions, I know his thoughts. We communicate through my speech or thoughts and his eyes, ears, body movements, barks, and growls.

I can understand why Native Americans believe in spirit animals and say they can talk to them. Sometimes, when my thoughts go back to Canada and the white wolf pup, Cocoa Corbuckas (which I sometimes call him) perks up his ears and stares at me. Animals have their own ways of communicating!

One day, I said, "Buck, we are two old dogs. We even have trouble getting in and out of the truck. Do you think we could hold up to make just one more trip back to Canada? Should we be just two old fools and give it a go?"

Cocoa perked his ears up and went, "*Rrwwoo.*" I guess that was the answer. He is game for any truck ride, near or far. He is a seasoned traveler now—having made six trips back and forth from Indiana to Arkansas, pulling a trailer behind the truck. Plus the trips Anita and I took to spend the summers.

So now, let's get this figured out. Canada requires a passport now, as well as a dog's history and current shots. We'll have to stop at Easter Day Avenue to get some money exchanged. We'll pack supplies and extra money.

Having completed all this, we headed out one pleasant Arkansas morning, heading for the North Country. We stopped at night for chow and to clean up and rest. Cocoa got his own bed at dog-friendly motels. We breezed through Canadian customs without too much trouble. The officer, who had a black lab at Homeland, was quite impressed with Cocoa, even if he was an old dog. We picked up Eleven East and headed for Little Rapids. We had an "in the truck stay" in Little Rapids, and the next morning, we headed north on the highway out of Little Rapids—a two-lane blacktop, actually.

When we reached the Last Stop petrol station with no power, I topped off the gas, got extra water, and other necessities. The wolf dog was no longer there. The years had taken their toll, and he was no longer alive, sadly! New people were running the store, and they had never heard about him. Sometimes, memories let time slip by you. It had probably been twenty years or more. I don't really want to know; I just want to live in the present.

Here and Now

"Well, Buck, we are here and getting close. It's been a very long journey. I can feel it in my bones now, and you look tuckered out. We will get up to Mountain Ash Lake before dark. If it's too late to get in or we can't get in, we will spend another night in the truck and see what we can do in the morning. Hopefully, no bears are on the prowl tonight because we don't carry a weapon. Sometimes, old duffers get a little stupid and think everything is just going to be fine."

We reached the Logging Road about dusk, with nightfall coming on fast. We opted for another night in the truck, planning to venture in when daylight would light our way. The night brought a gentle cool breeze and nothing but the sound of the night creatures singing their songs. Cocoa settled right to sleep in his backseat, and I wasn't far behind.

Good Morning, Ontario!

Cocoa wanted to go out, which started the day. I cautioned him to stay close and not to chase anything. The day was beautiful with big puffy clouds in a clear blue sky. There was a cool breeze, and life was good. It was time to move out. We started on the Logging Road, and it wasn't too bad. We took it slow and easy; with the brush and tight curves, caution was necessary. We came across a small flow of water across the road, a sign that the beavers were still at work damming the water.

As I proceeded slowly, my thoughts drifted back to Glen, and I whispered to myself, "Glen, old boy, I wish you were here on this journey with us." Then I thought of Anita. Would she be offering instructions or sitting in tense silence? A broad curve appeared ahead, leading to another. I could see the creek running below.

"Not far now, Cocoa," I said. Another turn revealed a trail heading down to a clearing. Amazingly, we had arrived, and the campsite was untouched by time. The pier looked as sturdy as it had when Glen was a young man. He and Evie had lived here in a cabin on this clearing. While working for Lands and Forest," Glen served as a fire spotter and had constructed a tower nearby. There was no electricity; they used a gas generator and a large fuel tank to power the cabin and charge batteries. They also had propane and cut wood for the stove and heating.

Every two weeks, a plane—likely a Beaver—landed on the lake, taxiing to the pier to unload supplies. Eventually, Forestry decided that the site was no longer needed. Glen transitioned to another job, and the Forestry department dismantled the Cabin Tower. Nothing remained except the pier, preserved for emergencies.

The old tower's location was up the trail: take a left turn and ascend the hill to reach the tower's base. From there, a one-hundred-foot climb led to the cab. Once inside, a person took their shift as a spotter, then descended the same distance at the end of the shift. Day in and day out, throughout the year. Now, all that remains of the old tower is the concrete base that anchored the structure. From that vantage point, if one can manage the climb, there's an unobstructed view above the trees, offering a spectacular panorama of the lake and surrounding area.

Camp Setup and Memories

Setting up camp was an easy chore since I only had a bedroll and camp utilities. So I started setting up right where Glen and I would camp. I noticed over at the edge of the woods the old outhouse was still standing in good shape. I thought that it was a good asset to keep a clean area. I built a fire ring out of rock. A little way into the woods, I saw a chinquapin (*chink-o-pin*) tree. Glen always used that tree for fire. It was one of the many trees still standing from when a large fire went through and destroyed the area years ago. These trees were left standing and bare. Glen said the Indians had called the trees chinquapin, but he didn't know why. They used these trees for firewood because they did not want to cut a good tree of the forest. The Indians were good stewards of the land.

As I looked around, I said to Cocoa, "A lot of good memories here, old boy! Long before your time and long back in my time, Glen would have thought you were a very fine dog, and he would take to spoiling." Quite a distance from here was where I took my fall and had an experience of a lifetime with a mother wolf and her cubs. I'll never forget them, and her white cub captured my heart in just that short time. Over the years, I had a lot of good memories, and I guess that was why I wanted to try a comeback one more time. It won't be the same, but I 'm thankful the beautiful surroundings have not changed."

So Cocoa and I settled in, and the next few days were a lazy life, walking and taking in the beauty of Mountain Ash Lake. We fished off the pier and caught a few small walleyes to cook on the fire and supplement our beef jerky and flatbread. I had a sack of feed for

Cocoa, but he most generally ate what I ate. My appetite had slowed down in my old age, and I just couldn't eat like I used to. I always told Cocoa, "I'll save you the last bite," and I did. Most always the last bite was half of my meal! At home, I always cooked for two—two old dogs!

The Visitor

One beautiful morning, Cocoa and I were kind of lazy and didn't get around right away. Cocoa gave a loud, rumbling growl, and I looked up to see a man in buckskin quietly walking into camp. In my laziness, I had just gotten the fire started. He came on in, and we looked at each other. He was Indian, dressed all in buckskin. In his headband were two feathers. Let me tell you about the feathers before I go on.

Feathers are an important symbol of the Indian way of life. In their culture, feathers are given as a sign of respect and honor and are held in high regard as they represent freedom, power, wisdom, honor, trust, and strength. For a native of a tribe who had a personal accomplishment or achieved something great for the tribe, to receive a feather is a sign of respect and honor. To receive a feather of any kind is considered a sacred gift—one that should be cherished and protected! So seeing the feathers, I knew he was a man of honor. And, to think, he had two!

The buckskin-clad man stood before me. On one of his sides was a tomahawk, and on the other side was a huge bowie knife. He was definitely not one you would provoke! After a few moments of staring at each other, a big smile with pearly white teeth came across his swarthy lined face. Then he said, "Good morning, Jim Gardner!"

I was speechless. I said, "How do you know my name?"

He said, "I have been watching and listening to you from nearby woods for one night and one day. For a while, your license plate confused me because it says Arkansas, and you are supposed to be from Indiana!"

"Well, there's a long story behind that," I said. "But now how do you know me?"

The broad grin again and he said, "We have a mutual friend, long passed now, Glen Brethour!"

"Wow," I said, and I noticed Cocoa wasn't a bit alarmed. "Yes," I said, "and Glen was my very best friend. We were like brothers."

And he said in return, "Our friendship was like brothers. If I ever needed him, he was there for me, and if he needed me, I was there for him. But we didn't interact much. He had his life, and I had mine. Now that you know me, you can call me James!"

He said, "My name is Mack-u-Tuc, but please, call me Eagle Feather." And wow! He had two!

I said, "I know the legend of the feather, so you must have done something of honor for your tribe. And who are your people?"

"My people are Ojibwe, and you passed through the reservation east of Sault Ste. Marie."

I asked, "Then how are you here? And will you be confronted by the Canadian Mounties for being here?"

Eagle Feather spoke, "I came here as a young man many moons ago! I cannot tolerate the reservation! I have lived all over this country. I used to be challenged by the law, but after a while, they grew tired and gave up! They now call me the eyes and ears of the forest. If there is a fire or trouble, I call the Forestry, and they notify the Mounties to assist at the scene."

I asked, "Well, how do you call them without a phone?"

Eagle Feather laughed and said, "No phone—I have an Indian phone!"

I asked, "Well, how is that?"

He said, "Well, in case of trouble, I go to clearing and build fire, then throw on green brush to make smoke. Then I take bedroll and wave over smoke and make signal. Soon, a fire spotter somewhere sees my smoke signal and immediately calls it into the Forestry. They will fly a Beaver over to assess the situation, then call Canadian Mounties and say, 'Your Indian is calling!' Then give ordinance, and they come!" Then he smiled and chuckled again.

Then Eagle Feather asked, "Why you here after all these years?"

I said, "One more journey to recapture old memories and see Mountain Ash for the last time."

Then he said, "You came for nine years and then no come back! Sad! Last trip with Glen. I heard you were called down by law for moving his body, but first phone was twenty miles back down! Besides, you are honorable man! You were bound and determined to take your friend home! That is good! Sometimes, white man doesn't understand honor! But you do good! Let me also say this. Glen was a good friend to me also! Glen also told me about your encounter with a female wolf and her pups! And you were quite taken with the white pup. You two could have easily bonded! I had a wolf dog, I know! He traveled with me many moons until old age took him down. I buried him in the forest. Wolf packs have been seen in the area, led by a big white male wolf, a dominant male! Now, I don't want to see you get worked up because it would not be your pup from long ago. Sometimes, memories get in our way! I say this to you as a friend! Too many moons have passed! A wolf's life span is about twelve to fourteen years. So there would have been three generations by now!"

I looked hard at Eagle Feather for a moment, and then I said, "Okay…three generations in the pup's life could produce a father to become a grandfather down to father. And then down to now a mature white wolf male whose lineage all reverted back to the wolf pup!"

Eagle Feather answered, "Maybe so, but unlikely. So even if you get to see this white wolf, don't let your heart get in the way, my friend."

To change the subject I said, "My fire is ready, and you are my guest. Come, put your bedroll down by my fire! Share my food, although meager. I hope you will stay for a while because we have a lot to talk about."

Eagle Feather said, "Maybe for a while."

Honored Guest

Eagle Feather put his bedroll by the fire. Then he asked, "Do you have a frying pan?"

I said, "Yes."

"Good. We'll go to pier and catch some fresh fish to go with your flatbread." At the pier, he threw out his hand line that he retrieved from his pack. I cast my pole. Before I got a bite, Eagle Feather had pulled in four nice walleye pikes. He said, "This is enough. Let's go cook. We eat. I'm hungry!"

So the days passed, and we enjoyed each other's company. We fished and ate our fill. Eagle Feather always left four on the stringer in the water by the pier. This could always be the next meal. He always left enough so Cocoa could get his share. He could fillet a fish quicker than you could blink your eye, and he was adept at cooking. Cocoa watched him as he cooked, looking for handouts, and the two were becoming close friends. I asked him if he missed his old dog, Keno. He said yes, he did. Then he said, "Maybe one day I will find another wolf dog in my travels. Maybe even a weaned wolf pup! Them being in the wild together would allow the pup to bond okay."

I asked, "Was your wolf dog like the one that used to come to the petrol station? He was a big fella, silver-gray, and had one brown eye and one steel-gray eye?"

He said, "Well, yes, pretty much. So I came across him in my travels. I guess he was abandoned."

I said, "Well, pup, can't leave you behind, so I guess you will have to travel with me. We bonded right away, and he became my constant companion for fourteen years. When he passed on, it was not from sickness. He died peacefully in his sleep. I buried him in a pretty spot in the timber. Like you with Cocoa, there. You always dread the day when it comes, but you have to go on. I guess it was better for him to go first because what would he do if I went first?"

I said, "I think about that a lot with Cocoa."

Then he said, "I believed that with him being mostly wolf, he might have reverted back to the wild, but then how would an old dog of fourteen make the transition? Really too old to cope with that life. As with you and Cocoa, life in an environment too adverse to revert back to his ancestors, and also too old to cope with it. I can see how he would be totally lost without you and probably grieve himself to death. Another person wouldn't know how to—or care to—take care of him the way you have."

I said, "Maybe it'd be best for Cocoa to go first and let me handle the grief, just like you had to do." We were silent for a spell, both knowing what the other faced or would have to face in the future. Then to change the subject, Eagle Feather asked me about Glen.

"Back to talking about Glen. Did he ever tell you how far the fire tower moved with the wind?" Eagle Feather chuckled at the thought.

"No, he never told me about that!" I said. "He told me all about the cabin and tower, but he never mentioned the sway!"

"You know?" he said. "Not exactly, but it could sway back and forth a greater distance than you could believe. It was designed that way to prevent it from snapping off in the wind!" He chuckled again and then said, "Knowing old Glen, when the sway started, it was probably naptime for him. You know, when the Forestry decided to retire that tower out of service, they put Glen on a 'mapping project.' From Mountain Ash down east to another mapping point. All this was charted territory. Glen, with an assistant, started from here and went down east where the map picked up. They had to walk that distance a little every day with instruments, follow coordinates laid out for them, and measure and report the lay of the land—describing the environment. Land falls, timber, lakes, streams, rocky mounts. And from that, map makers would use the information to work with and come up with a reasonable map of the area. They hiked this for so many hours of the day, then called in their location. When supplies were needed, a plane would go to the point they called in and drop supplies with a parachute. They better be very close with their position."

I said, "No, I never heardabout that story. I imagine there are many stories about Glen Brethour that we will never know."

Eagle Feather remarked, "Rightly so." We fell into a pattern, and every day, we took care of things that were needed and shared many stories and memories.

Then one morning, Cocoa whined to wake me up. When I looked, Eagle Feather was gone—bedroll and all. I was really upset. But then I had to admit that life was good, and after all, as an Indian, he had his ways and his lifestyle.

The Return

Cocoa and I poked around and did what we had to do. On day one, about dusk, we heard the wolves in the nearby timber. Cocoa set up a low growl that transitioned into a mournful howl. I said, "Quiet, Buck." I listened. Then emerging from the distant timber, appeared the big white wolf that everyone was talking about. He stood for a long time, and we exchanged prolonged glances. Cocoa couldn't take his eyes off him. Then as quickly as he appeared, he vanished back into the brush. The pack seemed closer now, yet I felt no fear. Cocoa and I went to bed as usual, with the fire stoked up pretty good. I thought, if need be, we could retreat to the truck. So these two old dogs drifted into sleep.

Day two brought some loneliness due to Eagle Feather's departure. I shouldn't have let that bother me. He had his life, and I had mine. I just didn't want to see a friendship disappear. Cocoa got me up bright and early in the morning. I stoked up the fire and decided to have a little bacon from our supply kit, along with some flatbread. After breakfast, I said to Cocoa, "I know it's a foolish move for two old dogs, but if we take it slow and easy, with rest stops, I'd like to go up on the bluff and check out the old fire tower site." Cocoa was ready to go. He always was. Until the last dog was dead!

The climb was slow, treacherous, and very tiring. But we made it, admiring the beautiful timber all the way up. In the clearing, we found the old foundation of the tower and sat down for a drink of water. I poured water into my palm so old Buck could get his drink. The view was spectacular! As far as the eye could see, Mountain Ash Lake lay below, immense and beautiful. The sun played off the riffles, making the whole lake shimmer as though it was sprinkled with diamonds. We soaked in the beauty, and I said, "This is Glen's world." Cocoa just looked at me. Many memories flooded my mind: life before, life after, and the memories I was creating now. Cocoa lay by my side, snoozing, and after a while, I suppose I drifted into a light sleep.

I don't know how long I napped, but when I awoke, I knew we needed to start our descent. "Come on, Buck. We gotta go!" The trip down was somewhat easier, and by the time we reached camp, the sun was dipping into the treetops, casting beautiful shadows across the campsite. "Well, old boy," I said, "no time for cooking tonight. I'll stoke up the fire, and then it's flatbread and jerky for supper." We spent a peaceful evening together, and then it was time to roll out the bedroll. Cocoa settled down by my feet, and we were alone. The howls of the wolves lulled me into a light sleep. Then I heard the rustle of brush. I cracked my eyes open slightly and saw the white wolf standing at the camp's edge, watching us. After a moment, he seemed satisfied and quietly retreated into the forest. All was well. Back to sleep.

The Encounter

The next morning, Cocoa stirred me awake as he usually does. I wanted to sleep in, but he was not about to have it. I got up, restoked the fire, and checked to see how my chinquapin wood pile was holding out. It was still in good shape. I got out my frying pan and said, "Real treat—bacon and flatbread for breakfast!" Cocoa didn't argue with that. There were times that he talked back with a *rwoooor*. This was his way of talking at times.

We went to the pier and tried our luck for a little walleye. That would make a good supper. It took some time; they were biting slowly, but in the end, there were two for supper and four on the stringer for later. I kept two tied in the water to keep them fresh for cleaning later, and they would be ready for supper's cook. Cocoa and I settled down, intending to have a "goof off" day.

Just as we were getting settled, I saw something moving on the trail. Cocoa saw me look, so he got up to investigate. He moved out of the campsite with a growl and a vicious bark as if he were on "duty" and wasn't going to tolerate any intrusion! He began heading down the trail. I yelled, "Buck, get back!" and I ran to catch up with him and contain him. I put my hand on his back and said, "Stay!" That noise was all it took because a huge black bear heard it and reared up. Bears have poor eyesight but keen hearing and sense of smell. He responded to Buck with a roar! He dropped down, beating his paws against the dirt. Then he reared up again, pawing at his chest, snarling, and slobbering at the mouth! Buck stood rigid, his hair on end, growling back, ready for a confrontation.

I thought, *Oh, crap! We bit the biscuit this time!* I stepped back, scanning the area for something to use as a weapon. I wished I had Eagle Feather's tomahawk and bowie knife to even the odds! Taking cover was out of the question, and we'd never make it to the truck in time. I knew Buck would never abandon the scene. For him, it was do or die. I didn't know what to do, but if the bear advanced, I would make as much noise as possible and hurl whatever was within reach. My primary concern was to ensure Cocoa didn't end up in the bear's clutches.

The bear was now rolling his head in anger. Slobber flew from his mouth, and his eyes looked as though they were on fire, resembling something from a nightmare. He began to move toward us, and I thought, *Hold your ground, Buck!* Then from the corner of my eye, I saw a flash of white. It was a white wolf emerging from the brush at the side of the trail! He approached the bear directly. His fur was bristled, his ears laid back, his head lowered, and his teeth (impressive fangs!) were bared, dripping with saliva. He slowly advanced, readying himself for an attack.

The bear stopped and dropped to all fours, eyeing the white wolf who was now moving in. The bear seemed to calculate the situation and must have decided that facing the large wolf wasn't worth the trouble. So he turned and trotted back up the trail. Once the white wolf had calmed down and regained his composure, he gave us a gentle look and then retreated into the brush, disappearing from sight. I was left speechless, overwhelmed, and grateful. I said, "Come on, Buck, let's head back to camp. No fighting for an old dog today. That could have been the end for both of us. You'd better make peace with that white wolf—if we see him again. He just saved our bacon!"

Friendly Return

Early the next morning, we had another visitor. Coming down the trail (friendly this time) was Eagle Feather! He had a stout pole across his shoulders, and tied off on each side were four large fish. When he reached camp, I couldn't wait to tell him the white wolf had been visiting. I recounted the night encounter and the episode with the bear. He looked at me in amazement. Then he said, "I'm glad I wasn't coming up the trail then with four fish swinging off my shoulders."

We laughed, and I said, "Well, maybe you could have fed him and calmed him down!" We both chuckled at that, and Cocoa joined in with his dog laugh. Then Cocoa went over and gave him a little nudge. Once everyone had settled down, I told Eagle Feather that I had something to say, clarifying that I didn't mean it in a negative way. "When I woke up and you were gone, I was upset. I didn't know what was going on!"

Eagle Feather responded, "I'm not good with goodbyes. They upset the heart. So my habit has been always to slip away."

"I can respect that," I replied, "but when it's time for you to go again, could you let me know the night before?"

He said, "Okay, I will do that because I know our paths will never cross again."

I responded, "That's true. And I want you to know what a special friend you've become to me. It will bring more good memories."

Eagle Feather paused and then said, "Friends, yes, but more like brothers. You will always be in my mind as I travel this land."

Back to Visit

I looked at the fish he carried in, and they were kokanee salmon. I hadn't had kokanee salmon since years ago when Glen and I fished them out of the stream at Little Rapids. Eagle Feather said, "I am anxious to tell more stories, more memories to share. And for me, the last story because it is about the white pup. I wasn't going to bring it up because you seemed worked up. So it will be the last story before we part. There comes a time when I have to move on and a time when you have to move on. But for both of us, it will be a good thing, not a bad thing. And I might add, a good thing for old buck here to go home and settle back, you two together."

I replied, "Yes, it has been an incredible journey."

Back to the Good Life

Eagle Feather said, "Now, I will get these salmon cleaned. We will have supper on me. I intend to smoke some for you and me to take on our departing journeys. Now, you can help. Get me some firewood, and we will start a separate fire from our campfire." He cleaned and prepared the fish down by the pier. The fire was started, so he cut two sturdy forked sticks and punched them in the ground on each side of the fire. He then cut a strong cross stick to lay across. After that, he gathered brush and made a brush arbor around the fire— not close enough to burn. Then he placed green sticks over the top to make a roof. He added a bit of green brush to the fire to produce smoke. After cutting the salmon into strips, he hung them over the cross stick. The smoker was on its way, and oh, the delightful aroma emanating from it!

For supper, we had cooked bacon, fried fish, and flatbread. Each of us had a share, and even Cocoa got his portion. With our bellies full and clean-up complete, we were ready to enjoy the evening. Every so often, Eagle Feather would check on his smoker.

Storytime

It turned into a beautiful evening as we sat around the campfire enjoying ourselves. Eagle Feather spoke up and said, "Tell me some stories about your visits with Glen."

I said, "Well, I'll try to get it straight, but over the course of the years, things, places, highways, cities, and whatnot have changed. Changed numbers, changed names, and even changed people. One trip I was on, Glen said to come up and meet his brother, Alden Brethour. They had just gotten back from Tobin Mary, where Alden was a lighthouse keeper on that island. He had to go back and forth by boat. Alden came back with Glen and Evie because he wanted to meet Glen's other brother—me, the Yank. While at Tobin Mary Island, Glen said it was small but beautiful. Everywhere on this island, you walked because of its size.

"On the day they were to leave and check things out, they started down stone steps to the shop. Glen was stopped by a coiled rattlesnake! He looked for a rock to kill it. Alden said, 'What are you doing?' Glen said, 'Looking for a rock to kill this bugger.' Alden said, 'No, wait.' And he went to the shop and came back with a wire cage box and a snake hook. He caught the snake and put him in the box that was crawling with rattlers! It seems they were abundant on that island. Glen said, 'What are you going to do with them?' Alden said, 'I take them ashore and sell them to a pharmaceutical company that makes serum.' Glen said, 'How are you gonna get them there?' Alden replied, 'In the boat with us when we leave.' Glen said it was the most nervous boat ride he ever had!"

It was time to turn in. Cocoa was already snoring! I told Eagle Feather that I would tell him another story tomorrow night. As things got quiet, we heard the wolf pack in the distance serenading the moon. There was a slight rustle in the brush. White Wolf had come for a look but didn't enter the camp. Eagle Feather motioned to me, and I turned to look. I was glad White Wolf had made an appearance for Eagle to see. I looked for Cocoa, and he had moved to a spot over by Eagle Feather.

In the morning, Eagle Feather was eager to talk about last night's sighting. He said, "He is getting bolder, and I believe you may be getting close to an encounter! That is why I told you it is time for me to leave and be traveling along. But tonight you will share another story about you and Glen. Then as I promised, I will tell you about my sightings of that white wolf."

With activities together again today, it was hard to think about Eagle Feather's departure. But this was his life and style. With supper over, Eagle Feather hurried about and built up the fire. He then took his seat around the fire, and with a grin, he said, "Okay. Storytime!"

I said, "Okay, my friend. Let me tell you about my Colburn Island trip with Glen. Glen called me and said, 'When are you coming up?' 'Soon,' I said. Glen went on, 'Evie and I are at Hector's camp on St. Joe Island. Hector asked me to get you up here because he has a little project coming up, and he needs our help!' 'Help with what?' I asked. Glen said, 'You know Hector. He won't tell you anything upfront but waits and springs it on you!' I had learned to go along with this. When I got to St. Joe, I spent a couple of days around the campfire with Glen and Evie. Then Hector arrived, and it was good to see him again. When Hector left that evening, Glen gave me the big announcement! At 6:00 a.m. sharp the next morning, we all were leaving on Hector's boat for Colburn Island. Well, Hector's boat was an old bugger with a cab over and bench seats on the sides. It had a big diesel marine engine that had plenty of power but no speed. Maybe eight knots per hour, and that was at full speed!

"At 6:00 a.m. we got underway. Hector said we were taking the bay water around the island to the main lake (Ontario). If the water was too rough, we would turn back and try it another day. When we rounded the cape, we ran into really rough water—swells and white-caps. Hector yelled, 'That's it!' and turned around to head in. When we docked, he said, 'See you folks in the morning, at six'

"The next morning, the trip out proved successful. A little fog, but Hector set his course by compass. After a long journey, Hector told Glen to get up on the bow and keep a lookout. There was a little island we had to pass around, and with the fog, it couldn't be seen! In a little while, Glen yelled, 'Island dead ahead, Hector, turn left now!' We passed the island, and Glen said, 'Okay, Hector, resume course.' Everybody was speechless for a moment. The fog started lifting, and we entered the calm waters of the bay at Colburn Island. What a beautiful sight the island was. I asked Glen, 'Who lived here?' 'Nobody,' he said. 'Years ago, when the timber mill went belly up, the people had to go back to the mainland to find work. One man from the township stays here, and from time to time is relieved. Upkeep and security for the island. When the people left, they just walked out of their homes and left. Later, in the years, the kids came back and took over the homes, and now it is a hunting camp. Years ago, the deer crossed the ice to here. Now we have a big deer population.'

"'How did the people get back?' I asked. He said, 'There used to be a ferry that ran back and forth from Debra to the island, but no more. If you come now, it's by private boat. There are no utilities now, no plumbing, no sewers, no electric. The man at the township building has a generator he can use. As a courtesy, he turns on the line to the houses, and you get one light bulb that goes on from 5:00 p.m. to 10:00 p.m., then off! You better be ready for you are in total dark!'"

Chores Again

"When we docked, Hector's brother Victor met us, and then the work started: unloading the boat for the island's needs. Full gas cans, oil, antifreeze, batteries, food supplies—all had to be carried to the house. I was relieved to see that Hector's house was the first one down from the township building. There were no slackers. Everyone pitched in to help. You had to, or you would face Hector's wrath. Victor told me to come and help him. We took fresh battery oil and gas to a garage by the house. Inside were an old pie wagon and a Dodge truck from the 1940s. We checked the battery oil and filled the gas tank, then added a little squirt of gas in the carburetor.

"Victor started cranking the engine. It cranked repeatedly. I thought to myself, that old engine isn't going to start. But then it caught. The engine coughed, ran roughly, and spewed smoke that filled the garage. After a moment, the engine smoothed out and purred. Victor looked up from under the hood and grinned at me. I asked if the vehicles had been left there, and Victor said, "No. We drove them over here on the hard ice in the winter.' I was amazed and asked, 'What if there was thin ice?' He replied, 'We drove around it! And if one didn't and went down? Oh well, one less' We loaded up water cans, and Victor said we were going to the community spring. As we drove on the gravel roads, Victor provided a thorough history of the island. At the spring, which had a protective cover, Victor removed it, revealing fresh water. We filled our cans. He mentioned that everyone respected the spring and took care to leave it as they found it—it was their water source. When we returned to Hector's house and unloaded the water, Victor remarked, 'I'll catch up with you later, ole buddy. I've got a few more chores to attend to' I knew better. That was his way of excusing himself. There was more work to be done."

The Surprise Request

"Hector's house was the only two-story house on the island. The upstairs was mostly two large bedrooms and a storage area. Antique beds, a dresser, and antique bedding looked as though they had missed several trips to the laundry. Old stairs led all the way down. The downstairs opened into the living room. A center wall with a door led into the kitchen. An old iron cookstove served for cooking as well as heating. There was an old sink and an eating counter, as well as an antique table and chairs. When I came down from upstairs, I saw Hector at the stove, engaged in conversation with four of his hunting buddies. Hector had the old black iron coffee pot steaming and a good breakfast coming off the cookstove.

"After breakfast, his buddies wandered into the living room. Then Hector announced, 'Fellows, I invited you here today to help with a little work project that will benefit us all.' Silence followed. 'With your help, and with Glen and his friend, we are going to remove the center wall between the kitchen and the living room!' He paused with a big smile on his face. The men just sat there, looking at each other. Hector continued, 'Glen's friend, Jim here, is an engineer and will head up this project! Now, Glen will be the crew boss, and you four gentlemen will be the grunts. So get your saws and hammers ready. There's a box of nails and a pile of strong sawmill lumber out back'

"Hector turned and looked at me. Oh, crap! I wasn't an engineer, but I wasn't about to rain on Hector's parade. So I addressed the crew 'Well, boys,' and they all looked at me as if to say, Who is this Yank calling us *boys*?'

"I began again, 'With further inspection of the building, I see that this center wall is not just a divider, but also a weight-bearing wall. So when you tear it out, you have to leave two two-by-fours in the center. If you don't, the upstairs will come crashing down.' I continued, 'When you remove that wall, leave those two two-by-fours in the center. It will stand. Then clean up the debris so you won't trip. Next, place a header on the living room side, setting it atop the two open ends. Afterward, you can remove the two center two-by-fours, and it will still stand. Lastly, place the other header on the kitchen side. Then you'll be done. You can add trim afterward if you wish.'

"Hector grinned and gestured, and the crew got to work with their hammers and chainsaws, and they carried in the lumber. Glen was barking orders. Once completed, the kitchen flowed into the living room. Hector remarked, 'Thank you, boys. Now, at Deer Camp, we won't have to chat through a door. We'll all be together in one great room.' While everyone was free to go, the men lingered, admiring their handiwork and deep in conversation.

"As for me, I took a stroll down to the beach for some quiet time. The beach boasted beautiful white sand that stretched as far as the eye could see. What was truly remarkable was the absence of any footprints in the sand—not from animals or humans—only the trail I left behind. The rest of my visit was delightful. Hector prepared delicious meals and kept the old black coffee pot brewing endlessly. Friday marked our departure, and the voyage back to St. Joe was scenic, marked by warmth, sunshine, and calm water."

Last of Storytime

Eagle Feather was quite taken with the stories, especially because they all surrounded my activities with his friend Glen! Then Eagle Feather went on to say, "Yes, this is the best visit I have ever had. Now you and I are another story." And he chuckled. Then becoming serious, he said, "I promised you I would tell the last story. After Glen had told me about your accident and encounter with the mother and pups visiting you in the night, from time to time I would see them. The mother took the pups and went back to the wolf pack. She fought her way in and became the dominant she-wolf. From time to time, I would see her running, and the sisters and white wolf growing in size and beauty. Then it was White Wolf always running at his mother's side, leading the pack.

After a while, when the sightings occurred, I noticed the mother was gone, and White Wolf was leading the pack. I assumed the mother had evolved into old age, as I was doing, and passed away. After that, White Wolf was always leader, then the sightings dropped off! Then after a while, I got reports from people around here. A wolf pack was on the move again, led by a big white wolf. Later, I saw it for myself—this big white wolf leading a new pack. So I thought that this new White Wolf I was seeing could have come down through the lineage of your pup. Grandfather to father to male pup! So that is the white wolf we are now seeing. Like I said, wolf years are about fourteen, and that puts it into our timeframe."

I took all of this into my mind, and it sounded logical, but I refused to be convinced. Then I asked, "Eagle Feather, do you believe in the Great Creator? Do you believe in the Great Spirit who watches over us and the animals of the forest?"

Eagle Feather was silent for a long time, staring at me. Finally, he spoke, "Yes, yes, I do, do you?"

And I said, "Yes, I do!"

And again, another pause, and he said, "You are a strange white man!"

I said, "Why so strange? The Great Creator formed us from the dust of the earth, and Indians believe that the Great Creator brought them from the earth. So the two beliefs run parallel! So we both came from the earth, so to speak, and we both have a Great Spirit, and I believe that everything is as one! But white man, in his greed, has failed to accept this!"

After Eagle Feather paused, thinking, he said, "Then we are brothers."

I said, "Yes."

Eagle Feather went on. "I have been thinking a lot about this, and I also want to share this with you. Many things are passing through my mind! I firmly believe that you will experience an encounter soon! My presence may hinder that. Although my heart says to stay, my mind tells me to go. I have enjoyed this paradise with you. Now, I need to move on to mine. So it's goodbye now, and I won't have to slip away in the morning. You, Buck, need to be alone right now. I feel that the answer will come to you both soon!"

I gripped his shoulder, and he gripped mine. I said, "I say goodbye to my brother. Safe journey, and I know our paths may never cross again! But this time together has brought me great joy in finding a good friend and my brother."

He refused the compliment. "The Creator should have made you an Indian! Because you have the belief and the love in your heart! Maybe someday, if we both stay good, the Great Creator will let our spirits walk together."

As I watched him walking back out the trail, I said to myself, "There goes a great man! They should have given him three feathers and not just two!"

The Encounter

After Eagle Feather left, the night air seemed to pick up. A little mist was in the air. I built the fire up good and big for the night. With the chill in the air, I knew that Cocoa would be exposed on his little pad. I went to the truck and retrieved his seat cover from the backseat. I put his pad on it and had him lie down, then I tucked it all around him like a nest. He was content. As I snuggled down in my bedroll, I could feel the chill in the air. Many things were on my mind. Finally, I drifted off into a deep sleep. Subconsciously, I felt the chill!

In the middle of the night, I felt a warmth on my back. I thought Cocoa had moved over. I quietly looked back. White Wolf was sleeping against my back! His big head was tucked in the back of my knees. I said, "Oh, dear Lord, thank you!" I returned to sleep, careful not to disturb him. I don't know how or why, but this was that white pup!

In the morning, Cocoa nudged me awake as usual, telling me it was time to get up. The white wolf had left in the night. I started to put Cocoa's cover back into the truck. Cocoa growled his low growl! I turned to look! White Wolf was standing on the edge of the camp-site! He started to walk back to the timberline. Then he came back to the edge of the campsite. He did this three times. Cocoa came to my side. I knew what he wanted—"Come with me!" It was so sad! Tears were welling up in my eyes.

"Oh, White Wolf, we cannot go with you! You are from the wild world. Cocoa and I are in a different world. We would not survive in your world, like you cannot survive in ours." Tears were streaming down my face now. I knew that when he turned this time, he would go! I knew it would be forever. I knew now that this was my long-lost wolf pup.

As he approached the wood line, I dropped to my knees. Cocoa came to my side, ears laid back! With tears streaming down my face, I yelled, "WHITE PUP—SPIRIT WOLF!" He stopped, turned around, lowered his head, ears back, mouth open like a half grin. Wagging his tail—wagging too hard! He came bounding back to me! He hit me hard and put me on the ground. He was licking my face and my arms and nudging me all over with his nose! With a yelp, Cocoa moved in, ears back and whining. White Wolf placed his big foot on Cocoa and started licking his face. Then he turned his attention back to me!

Abruptly, he arose and returned to the wood line. I knew now, without a doubt, this was my white pup, grown now, and somehow, he had turned into Spirit Wolf! I knew that this was it. He would enter the forest never to be seen again. I called, "Spirit Wolf, I will never leave you! Sometime, in a different realm, I will walk with you! My spirit will walk with your spirit, and Cocoa's spirit will be with us." Spirit Wolf blinked his eyes, wagged his tail, and disappeared into the timber.

As I stood there, silent, Cocoa came to my side and nudged me. I looked at him and said, "Cocoa, you never saw the beginning with the white pup, but you have seen the end with the white wolf! This has gone full circle now, and may the circle never be broken!" After a few moments, I said, "Okay, Cocoa, let's break camp. It's time to go now. Time for two old dogs to go home!"

The Quest
for Quanah

A story from the imagination

James A. Gardner

THE QUEST for

QUANAH

Ima

Introduction

I am about to bring you a story from the figment of my imagination. There may be some facts that are partly correct, but none that could hold me accountable. It is a fictional story about thoughts in my mind and for my fascination and respect for our Native Americans. The white man calls them indigenous or Indian. Some Native Americans are not too pleased with that terminology. They like to be referred to by their tribal name or as "the people." To facilitate less writing, I will, in a polite manner, use for identification—Indian, tribal name, or people.

My fascination for the Native Americans (Indians) heightened when I bought a book about Quanah Parker from the library in the Cowboy Museum located in Oklahoma City, Oklahoma. From this book, and also many internet references, you can get the true facts about Quanah Parker, his family, his life, his deeds, and his later accomplishments. It is factual, historical, and an exciting read. From this story, I can only give you excitement from the depths of my imagination!

Some writers write in the second or third person. I will be writing this story in a slightly different fashion. I will be writing with the spirit of myself, about what is in my imagination! Have I lost you yet? You may say, "This guy is a nutcase!" but, my dear reader, I have to do this for the story's ending, and you will understand when we get there. Thanks. In the prologue, I hope to give you a sketch of Quanah Parker. So let's get on with this story!

The Beginning

In the mid-1800s, I was a young man from the East—a loner, non-conformer, and one without direction. Some folks would say I was "a rebel," some would say "a little rough around the edges." I was one who did not like to see people put down or abused. Also, with all this uncertainty, I was unsure what I wanted to do with my life. I lived near the banks of the Delaware River, and I liked being there for the solitude, peace, and quiet, and watching the tides coming in and going out. There was a lot of history there: the remains of Fort Billings and, further up the riverfront, Red Bank, two prominent places during the Revolutionary War. It was also home to the Delaware Indians who camped there along the banks. They were mostly driven out by then, moving west, with just a few stragglers remaining. I used to dig in the dirt of the bluffs and hunt for artifacts and arrowheads.

One old Indian preparing to move out had a few horses, mustangs specifically. I had my eye on a beautiful buckskin stallion. I tried several times to persuade the old fellow into selling me that mustang, but he wouldn't budge. Now that he was preparing to move out, I negotiated with him again. I had some money from the "odd jobs" I worked. Being a jack-of-all-trades came in handy to pick up work. After some haggling, we settled on a price I thought I could handle. I said, "It's a deal if you throw in the tack!" I suspected by the looks of it that he probably acquired it under dubious circumstances. So the deal was struck: he had money to head out, and I had a fine horse and tack. Since he was a beautiful buckskin, I named him

Buck. It didn't take long for Buck and me to bond, and with some patience, he responded well to my training.

Now back to the Delawares. There were a lot of stories about them—some true, some not. As they were pushed out and traveled west, they caused a lot of havoc! Along their way, they would attack settlers, kill them, and take food or anything else they wanted.

One family in particular, the Slocums, were attacked. The boys ran and hid, while little Frances, the girl, had to stand by and watch her mom and dad meet their death. The Delawares scooped her up and took her along as hostage. I heard that as they were moving through a place called Indiana Territory, they dealt her off to a Potawatomi Tribe that lived along Mississinewa River. Now, these people were good, peaceful. They farmed and fished. Frances Slocum was assimilated into the tribe, grew up with them, learned their ways, and eventually married and had children.

So the story goes, the boys grew up, and then for years they searched for their sister. Going by hearsay and reports from folks, they finally came across her. She remembered them, and it was a joyful reunion. They wanted to take her back, but she refused no matter how hard they tried to persuade her. This was now her life. She grew up their custom and ways. She married, had a good husband, and had his children. She was not going to go; she was going to stay with her people. This event really fueled my fascination, and I was hooked. I had to know more about these people.

The River Rat

One of my few friends was an old duffer who lived along the river. He lived alone and was always searching up and down the river beach for any treasures that would come in with the tide. Out of respect, I did not refer to him as a River Rat. Most folks did—that's how they referred to the people who lived along the river. This was another pet peeve of mine—people's disrespect.

I never knew the old boy's last name and didn't really have a need to. His name was Neil, and that was what I called him. Neil became like a grandpa to me, and we hit it off right away! Now, Neil always carried his rifle on his journeys. There might be a chance to run across a rabbit or see a squirrel on the run. For him, this was supper in the pot and, maybe, leftovers.

Neil became excited about my horse and how I came about getting him. He was also impressed by how we bonded and how I had him trained to strict obedience. I trained not with harshness but with love! He knew that I was getting closer to the "quest" that I told him about. Now, Neil was a marksman with his rifle. That's what impressed me and drew me into this friendship. One day, he pulled a coin out of his pocket and told me to place it on a log down yonder and then get back here to a safe place. I did as I was told and gauged the distance to 200 yards on the way back. I came back laughing and said, "Now, don't tell me you intend to hit that coin! At 200 yards!"

Neil said, "Yes, that's what I'm gonna do, and your job is to keep an eye on that coin and where it goes."

I said, "Man, I can't even see the coin!"

He said, "You will see it when it flies, so keep an eye on where it lands! Now get to looking."

Neil took position—relaxed—checked his breathing—took careful aim and made an easy pull on the trigger. Wham! I saw the coin fly! It hit the sandy beach. I ran to retrieve it while it was still in my sight, and darn if he didn't hit that coin dead center! Then he was quiet for quite a spell, and I knew he was pondering something.

When Neil spoke, it was serious. "Are you still gonna go out West and hunt them Indians?" He was getting me excited.

He continued, "Then you need to go down Texas way. A place called Fort Sicc. They've been trying to catch a renegade half-breed called Quanah. His momma was like that Slocum girl—carried off in a raid of Fort Parker. It could become a long search because those Comanches controlled everything from East Texas maybe clear north to the Dakotas! They even got a little of the Lakota-Sioux land but let those folks join up with them."

By now, I was so pent up with excitement that I could pop! "How do you know all that?" I asked.

Neil replied, "I am an old man. I've been around for a long time." I was ready to rattle off some more.

Neil said, "Calm down a minute, son! We've got some talking to do if you're serious."

"Yes, sir, I am!" I exclaimed.

Then Neil said, "Listen up. We've got some work to do. I'm gonna teach you how to shoot that coin, then we're gonna teach that horse of yours to hold steady when you have to shoot while mounted."

"Heck, Neil, I don't even have a gun!" I protested.

He reassured, "Don't you worry about that right now. Get ready, we start tomorrow!"

Neil was already there when I arrived early. He had brought his lever-action, high-powered rifle, which I could see was a precision piece. He said, "We will do extensive training with the .22-caliber rifle, and when you are proficient, we will switch to the Winchester. Ammo is too expensive to shoot up the big caliber."

I was already pretty good with my little .22-caliber pump, but I held my tongue. I wasn't about to interfere with Neil's program. Neil continued, "After I get you where I want you, we will start working with your horse, Buck. Along with shooting, we will also, per my demands, be able to break down these rifles, clean, and reassemble them. In the dark if need be!"

I was amazed, and I had to ask, "Neil, where did you ever learn to do all this?" Neil was quiet for a bit, and then he replied, "I'll give you a quick answer, and you better keep this to yourself and not tell anyone. I was a precision shooter in the military!"

I didn't respond, but I thought, *And this man, whom the people around here call a river rat, they don't realize to what lengths he went to preserve their freedoms*

Training went well, and I felt that I was becoming proficient. And Neil said I was! Even Buck got a passing grade. His training was to "hold steady" when I fired a rifle across his head. He, once trained, never flinched when I pulled the rifle out of the scabbard and said, "Steady, Buck." In the following days, we spent quality time together and enjoyed life in general. I was becoming eager to head out, and Neil sensed it. One morning, shortly before I left, Neil arrived carrying that Winchester and some ammo. He thrust the rifle into my hands. Stunned, I asked, "What's this about, Neil?"

He replied, "Well, son, I think you'll need this. I'm getting older, and I don't have anyone to pass this down to. So I guess I want you to have this You are the right person."

With tears in my eyes, I couldn't find the words, so I embraced Neil.

Heading Out

I was ready to go, and Buck was ready to move out! I tested him one more time. I pulled the Winchester out of the scabbard and said, "Steady, Buck!" He pulled up and stood perfectly still, and I praised him for his performance, and we moved out.

Like I said, I was a young man in the 1800s and was seeking a direction in my life. I wanted to follow my dreams! I had heard stories about the West and the Indian battles, and I wanted to go there! I heard a lot of stories about a leader called Quanah from Neil, and I wondered to myself. With Neil being in the military, was it possible that he had been there? Like the Francis Slocum story, Cynthia Ann Parker was abducted in an Indian raid on a place called Fort Parker. The Comanche were angry because the settlers were killing off all the buffalo. As the story goes, she was also assimilated into the tribe called Nokoni, and when she grew up, she married a chief called Peta Nocona. Just to think, she was only ten years old. I wonder if the Slocum girl was ten? Cynthia Ann was mother to Quanah and two other siblings. She was known to have two additional children.

Cynthia Parker raised her son, Quanah. He was blue-eyed, carried his father's features, and it was known that the siblings called him a "blue-eyed half breed." From what I've learned from hearsay and stories, he was raised in the culture of the Comanche. He could speak fluent Comanche, as well as English. This must have been through his mother. As Quanah grew up in the Quahadi camp (which was a branch of the main Comanche), he was more or less mocked by the Comanche youth. Pushed aside, so to speak. All of these things by talking to various individuals who were familiar with the situation surrounding the history of the Comanche nation. It was said that Quanah had the determination to overcome this, and as he grew in strength and wisdom, he was soon superior to the youth in the camp.

As he emerged as a young warrior, he excelled beyond them and was soon accepted as the leader of the Quahadi band (known as Antelope), a band of the main Comanche. He rose in the ranks as a strong warrior, the leader of this section of Comanche. His fame was now known, especially to the army. He became a thorn in the side of the military. All of this history was rolling around in my head on the long journey west, and it was a long, grueling trip from the East to the West. I was hoping that my journey was not in vain and that I surely would come in contact with more people in the know that could add to the story. Finally, I met some travelers heading east to settle near the Arkansas River. They assured me that Fort Smith was not too much further and that I should stop and rest a spell. I could also replenish my supplies. I had no supplies, so to speak, a bedroll and some deer jerky that Neil had prepared for me to take on the trip.

Fort Smith sounded like a good stopping point. The travelers said there were always a lot of folks at the fort who were coming and going, civilians and military who might be able to lend more information about the Comanche movements. So Fort Smith it was. Buck and I were both worn down from that long journey from the East.

Fort Smith was a buzzing beehive. A mix of military, civilian, trappers, and traders—a big mix of everything. It was the crossroads from the East to the West. Everyone was heading somewhere. There was even a wagon train heading out of the fort setting a course north for the Nebraska Territory. Everyone with a destination and too busy to talk! One night would be good enough for me, and Buck looked anxious to get out of the confusion.

Back on the Trail Again

It was warm and breezy. The good weather made me feel more confident. After the long journey out, we traveled for many days, not seeing more than the landscape. One midday, I saw a wagon train moving ahead, going west. My pace allowed me to catch up to it without much effort. Buck and I trotted forward to the lead wagon and caught the wagon master's attention. He called for a "pullup" and let the folks rest. Then he said, "Howdy, young man. What brings you to these parts?"

"Same as you," I said, "heading west."

The wagon master said, "We are heading for Fort Sill—where are you heading?"

"Same place," I said.

The wagon master said, "Well, you can ride along with us… We might come in need of that rifle you are carrying there."

I said, "Will do. I'm getting a little hungry anyhow."

So I went along, and the folks on the train were good people. They all shared in order to feed me well. That was a far cry better than jerky for a while.

Seven days into the journey went by, and one day the scout came trotting and bucking. He told the wagon master that, ahead, just over the rise, there were buffalo grazing. The wagon master called a halt and told the people to make camp for now. Then he, Scout, and I rode out. When we came to the rise, I climbed to the top and looked at the herd grazing below. "Stay quiet here, and let me slip down quiet-like, slow and easy and see if I can get in range. They may not spook if they see a horse grazing a little." So I eased out my

Winchester and started Buck downhill. Nice and slow, we went. I gave Buck his head and let him graze a little on the grass. The buffalo flinched, but when they saw the horse coming slow and grazing in the distance, they went back to grazing. When I was about 200 yards from them, I said, "Steady, Buck," and took my aim on a big buffalo staggering behind. Down he went with a clean shot, and so did the herd, thundering out of there!

The wagon master said to Scout, "Go back and bring Ajax. We got to field dress this animal." When Ajax came, he was riding his mule, whom he called "Henry." I looked in amazement. Here came this little, gnarly old man on this mule, and I thought: the names should have been switched. The mule should have been Ajax, and he should have been Henry! Nonetheless, old Ajax knew his business. He field dressed that animal in nothing flat. He then told us to give him our ropes, and he and Henry would get that "bugger" back to camp.

He then told the wagon master, "Tell the folks we will be here for a spell. I want each wagon to prepare a clean cloth to wrap their portion. I want a fire started and the folks to 'turn to' and start gathering firewood to go through the night." Then Ajax and Henry went plodding off back to camp. With instructions obeyed, there was a good fire going soon. First, Ajax cut a good portion for supper. Everyone had a good feast that night! Then he carefully skinned the hide in place. I thought I could help him on that, so I got up and went over. He said, "Go back over there and sit down, sonny. I can handle this." With the hide laid back, he scraped it clean, and it started to dry. This gave him a clean surface to work on. I kept the fire going with sticks while the folks were gathering more firewood. Then Ajax cut a portion for each wagon in the group. He then seared or burnt each portion until it had a burnt crust! Then he laid each portion on one of the clean cloths.

I thought the old man was screwing up, so I asked, "What are you burning the meat for?"

He said, "I ain't burning it! I'm preserving it! You see—with that hard crust, that meat can go a week and still be good under that crust. In cool weather, it can go two weeks wrapped in these cloths."

"Where did you learn that?" I asked.

"Peru," he said. I questioned that. I had no idea what he was talking about! He said, "When I was a young man, I was invited to go into Peru on a search for a hidden city in the jungles. The natives prepared the meat this way for our journey."

I said, "Well, did you find the city?"

Ajax smiled and said, "Hell no! But we ate the meat." Then he chuckled to himself.

I sat there thinking, *Boy, this old man is a class act!* I went into the night sitting around the fire, telling stories with the old man. He cut strips of meat and smoked them, a portion for each person or family in the wagon train. Then he made jerky. A portion for each wagon.

Then he asked, "What can I prepare for you, young man? It was you who brought this animal down."

I said, "A little jerky to replenish my supply would be fine. I've been eating off the wagon train folks for a spell." So Ajax replenished my jerky supply.

As we watched the fire burn low for the rest of the night, Ajax got around to asking me where I was headed and why. I told him that I was interested in an Indian leader named Quanah. I had some history and stories about him, and I wanted to go in search to try to find him. Ajax just raised an eyebrow at that comment! I paused for a moment and then told him the area I came from out East was fluent with the Delaware Tribe at one time. Then I told him the Frances Slocum story. I related how a similar incident occurred with Cynthia Ann Parker, kidnapped by the Comanche band at the Fort Parker Raid. She was ten years old at the time and was raised in the tribe. She matured, married a chief, and bore and raised three children. One of the children was Quanah. I just had this urge to go and find him. Fascination, I guess, or to satisfy myself. The stories got me worked up to make this pursuit! Then I asked Ajax if he could contribute anything to the story.

He said, "Yes, I know a little about what you said and what I have learned. The army hates him, you know. He became a leader of the Quahadi band. Commonly known as the Antelope people. He was born in the Kokoni band. Son of Peta Nocona, Comanche chief. I guess you know that the Comanche are made up of many bands, thereby being part of the greater Comanche nation, and they control everything from Texas to the Dakotas. I heard that Quanah is a rising star in leadership against the army. The army calls him the blue-eyed half breed…among other things! He is a thorn in their side, and they have developed a strong hatred for him. The army can't capture him, and they can't defeat him. He wins every battle they get into. So I think what you have in mind, young man, you better reconsider. You won't find him, but he will surely find you if he hears of your quest! Watch your back. It's like hunting a rattlesnake in the rocks. He's gonna get ya."

Moving On

The long journey with the wagon train was coming to an end. With Fort Sill in sight, I caught up with the wagon master and thanked him for the journey together before we got separated in the fort. He said that Ajax had told him about my intentions. He said, "When we get to Fort Sill, our paths separate. I don't know where your paths will lead, maybe into a whole passel of trouble? Our path now will go north. These folks on the train want to go to Nebraska and get a piece of ground and become sod busters. Think your situation over. If you have a change of mind, you are more than welcome to come along with us to Nebraska. Maybe you would find a little something there to your liking?"

I said, "Thank you. Just the same, but my quest is still pulling at me, and I want to pursue it."

As a loner, I wasn't too pleased with Fort Sill. The folks were not too friendly. The soldiers were brawlers and drinkers. The trappers and hunters were about the same. I went to the fort supply and looked for a few things that I might need on my travels. I ran into a sergeant major who was assigned to the fort. I struck up a conversation. I thought I might get a little information from him. I asked about Quanah Parker. His response was, "What do you want to know about that half breed for?"

I said, "Curious, I guess… where would I find such a man if I had a reason to?"

He said, "You don't have to find that one! He would cut you up in strips, smoke you, then have you for supper!" Then he continued,

"The army can't even find him or catch him. If they get close, he comes out from nowhere like a guerrilla fighter and defeats them!"

I asked, then, "Well, where is his territory?"

The sergeant major just looked at me for a few moments then said, "The Comanche nation's territory extends from the Apache nation's territory, down by Old Mexico clear up through Texas, Oklahoma, north up to the Dakotas. The Comanche nation has already taken the Sioux lands. But they allowed the Sioux to stay on the land. They would be used as allies in times of need."

I said, "Thank you, Sergeant Major, for your information. Although it sounds crazy, Quanah will still be my quest, whether I succeed or fail, taking the risk of living or dying!"

The sergeant major looked at me and said, "Young man, are you crazy?"

"No, sir," I said. "It's like something in my crawl, and I've just got to attempt to do it. I need to put this thing to rest."

He said, "I see you have a persistent determination, and it's going to be do or die! If you are going to insist on this, my advice would be to backtrack to the Oklahoma Indian Territory, the Wichita Mountain Area. He seems to take refuge there from time to time until he is rooted out for another battle."

So in a few days, I gathered up a few supplies, saddled my Winchester, took my bedroll, and saddled up. Then Buck and I headed out for the longest journey and the biggest pursuit of fantasy I had ever had in my lifetime! As I traveled across the country toward the forest and mountain country, I wondered if I would ever find what I was looking for or if this was just a "fool's folly." Then I said to myself, "James, what have you got yourself into now?" Then I said, "Come on, Buck—long trail ahead!" And old Buck moved on with a little spring in his step like he was enjoying all this. Finally clearing the foothills to the Wichitas, I came upon a peaceful stream winding through the beautiful forest. It seemed deathly quiet, and up ahead I saw smoke slowly drifting up through the trees. I said to myself, "Must be an encampment somewhere up ahead."

The Princess

Just as I rounded a bend in the trail, I saw an Indian maiden washing some of her things in the stream. I whispered, "Steady, Buck," and he stood perfectly still. I watched her for a long time and was absolutely mesmerized by her beauty. She was so beautiful that it took my breath away! After a spell, I thought I should softly speak to get her attention so as not to frighten her. Before I could speak, she turned and was shocked to see me sitting there. I smiled, and then she smiled the most beautiful smile I had ever seen.

Before I could utter a word, simultaneously she was gathering her things and scurrying up the trail. At the same instant, I felt three sharp points in my back. I sat still and did not look back until the maiden was scurrying up the trail toward an encampment. I risked a look behind me, and three braves were holding drawn bows against my back. One brave who could speak my language motioned for me to get down.

He spoke, "Move on to the camp, white eye!" So move on to the camp, I did!

I asked, "What do you intend to do with me?"

He said, "No talk—just go!" He and one brave kept their bows drawn against my back, and the third was leading Buck in. When we got to camp, they stripped Buck of his tack and laid my belongings down by the roped-off area containing their mustangs—mares, geldings, and stallions. Then they put Buck in with the group. I looked as he went in, and he was elated! A whole new group of friends! He could whip any stallion in there and court whoever he pleased!

I said, "Thanks, Buck!" The three braves tied my wrists in front of me and tied a long rope around my neck, attaching the other end to a pole in the center of the clearing. I received many hostile looks from the camp's residents, especially the old women. I wasn't going to show fear, so I looked with an angry face at the brave who could speak my language.

"Now what?" I demanded.

He looked at me with contempt and said, "In time, the chief will come to speak with you! He wants to know why you're here and what your intentions are with his daughter!" I expected someone to come. For three days, I waited, hands bound, neck sore from the rope tied to the pole. I slept on the ground. Each day, two old women came to give me a drink. It was hot. One day they brought me a bowl of some kind of gruel to eat. With my hands bound in front of me, I could hold the bowl and slurp from it. At least it was clean! The bowl was made from some kind of polished gourd. When I had to relieve myself, I turned away from them and did the best I could with bound hands, under the scrutiny of hostile faces. To sleep at night, I had to get close to the pole on the ground so the rope would not tug at my neck. I did a lot of thinking, and one thought was: what was going to happen to me next? I began to think that this quest was not going to turn out well! But I wasn't going to cry out, I wasn't going to give in. I was going to be brave. Along with that, I was going to stay angry!

Quanah

On the fourth morning, the chief finally emerged from his teepee. He stared at me, and I at him. My "quest for Quanah" had come full circle! We stared at each other for a long time; then I spoke first in anger. "You! You were supposed to talk to me, give me an audience! How dare you leave me tied to a pole like a dog! Gray and thirsty and having to piss in the dust. Waiting for big chief Quanah to come out to speak! Big chief 'unpolite' Quanah, I might add! I know who you are, Quanah! The one I have sought!"

Quanah raised an eyebrow and was silent for a spell. Then he spoke, "You are brave, white man, to speak to me like that! To speak to me in bad words and angry face while being tied to a pole like a dog! Why are you here, white man, to come to kill great Quanah and become a great hero among the Whites?"

I softened my voice and said, "No, Quanah. I came hoping to see if I could join you. I could be loyal to you and prove to be an asset."

He was silent for a moment, then asked, "Tell me why you, a white man, want to come and mingle with the Comanche?"

I said, "Several reasons. I have respect for you. I am a loner, and I know what kind of life I want. I don't want the white man's stealing of land and destruction of land when he gets it. I hate greed; I hate the slaughter of innocent people. I love this land that the Great Creator has given us. I want to live upon this land and be a great steward of it. I want to live on the land, free and happy!"

Quanah was silent for a while, then spoke, "Well said. But one more thing! What were your intentions when you came upon my daughter?"

Then I spoke, "I would not have harmed one hair upon your daughter's head! I did not know at the time that she was your daughter, only until now when you just spoke. When I came upon her on the trail, her beauty was so precious that I was smitten. I was so mesmerized that I could not speak. Before I could, they brought me in! Now that we have cleared the air, I did not know that was your daughter! I was going to ask whoever her family was if I might ask for her hand in marriage! That was not my quest on my search for you, but now that both have occurred, I ask if I may join your cause, and, if remotely possible, have your daughter's hand in marriage?"

Quanah raised his eyebrow again and looked at me. He said, "Comanche don't ask for a woman's hand in marriage. They ask for her heart!" He was silent for a moment, then turned and looked at the tent opening and said, "Beating Heart…did you hear all of that?"

The beautiful princess emerged from the teepee and said, "Yes, Father, I have heard." Quanah stayed silent for a spell and let us look at each other. She was clean and beautiful, and I was dirty and stank from my three days on the pole. She smiled at me like an angel, and I thought, what could she possibly be thinking about something like me before her that looked like this?

Her eyes twinkled, and she asked, "What is your name?"

Even Quanah had not asked my name! I answered her, "My name is James."

Then she smiled again. "My name is Beating Heart, named by my father."

I said, "I feel ashamed to be in your lovely presence in the condition I am in."

Beating Heart then smiled and said, "I see you as the handsome man who approached me quietly on his horse!" I stayed silent.

Then Quanah spoke, "Beating Heart, what are we to do with this thing before us? Do you want this dog tied to a pole?"

Without much hesitation, Beating Heart said, "Yes, I will take the dog tied to a pole." Then she giggled.

Quanah then tried to discourage her. "Even to marry? He asked for your heart!"

Beating Heart replied with one word, "Yes!"

Quanah was quiet for a spell, then he spoke, "My daughter is tugging at my heart! When she was born, I lifted her to my face and heard her little heart beating strong! So I named her Beating Heart. I love her very much, and I don't understand what is going on here. Only the Great Creator knows all things in people's lives, but I will have to give my blessing to two things. Yes, you can join me, James, and yes, you can marry my daughter. But, in order to do this, it is Comanche custom that you have to become blood brothers. Beating Heart, are you willing to perform this ceremony with this man?"

She said, "Yes, I am ready."

My ropes were cut, and Beating Heart was put before me. My bonds were cut, and Quanah became the medicine man. He stepped forward and spoke to Beating Heart in my tongue. "Give me your wrist." Then he took his knife and made a small slash on her wrist - enough to draw blood. Then he looked at me and said, "Give me your wrist!" Again, he slashed enough to draw blood. Then with elbows bent and forearms together, we clasped hands until our wrists touched. Then he bound us together with a strip of hide. Then Quanah spoke, "As the blood of these two flows together, his blood into our Comanche blood, this man becomes a blood brother of all our people. All Comanche must note, and, with respect, receive him. And let it be known that this blood that has been intermingled was from the strong blood of my daughter.

Then Quanah spoke and said to me, "Now that you are my brother and I agree to give consent to you marrying my beloved daughter, what do you have to say to Beating Heart?"

I looked into Beating Heart's eyes, the most beautiful eyes on earth, and said, "I know the time between us was short, but I loved you when I first saw you. I love you now, and I always will. Together we will face life, have our children, and I will help you raise them in the ways and customs of the Comanche! I will never leave you until the end of time, and not even then if it is the will of the Great Creator."

Then Beating Heart looked into my eyes and said, "I love you, and I always will. Yes, we still have our children and raise them in the Comanche way. I love you dearly, and I have prayed to the Great Creator to send me someone like you! I have hoped and waited many moons. Now you are here! We will have children and raise them in the Comanche customs, and I will teach you those spiritual ways. I, in turn, want you to teach me your ways. Also I will teach our children to speak the Comanche tongue and also teach them your tongue!"

Prepare for Ceremony

Quanah told two braves to take two older women and me back to the stream and clean me up for the wedding. I stank! Of course, I would get the two older ones that fed me while I was tied to the pole!

So the two braves accompanied me back, this time without weapons in my back and with some respect. The two older women did not have on angry faces now but laughing faces. I wondered why it had to be four people to give me a bath. But when we got to the stream, the two old women stripped me down and pushed me into the stream, laughing and giggling the whole time. They laughed and pointed at my white body shivering in the water, and then they gave me a good scrubbing, and believe you me, they missed nothing. I thought the game was taking a little long! I smelled smoke, and when I turned to look, the two braves had emptied my pockets and were burning my clothes! What now? Am I going to have to walk buck naked in the wilderness?

Then the old women picked me out of the water and started to dry me off, rubbing me down with a light blanket. Then when I tried to help out, they said, "No—Quanah's orders!" There on the bank lay what I was to wear. A new pair of fancy deer hide britches and a top to match. Everything was handmade, fringes and all! There were colorful designs woven in and dyed designs. There was a pair of new handmade moccasins for my feet. I gathered my personal stuff, and we headed back to camp.

Wedding Ceremony

Quanah started the proceedings with Beating Heart and me standing before him, and all the people gathered around. He started a prayer to the Great Creator for blessings for this union before Him, this man and woman. He gave thanks for His hand in our lives and asked Him to grant us a long life with much love and love to return back to Him. He gave thanks for all the good spirits in the woods and under the guidance of the Great Spirit who attended to all things.

Then we were greeted and hugged by all. I was happy I was alive, and now my wife was the most beautiful person I had ever laid eyes on. Dressed in her best regalia, she started her wedding dance, and soon all the people joined in. There was feasting, tribal ceremonial dancing, and all-around good sharing. We stayed late, but when we saw that things were not going to slow down, Beating Heart and I slipped off to her teepee to consummate our marriage. As I lay there with the most beautiful woman in the world in my arms, I thought—just a few hours ago, I was a beaten man, stinking and angry, tied to a pole like a dog. Not knowing what was to become of my princess! My thoughts went back to the wagon master when I told him I had to find my destiny. Now…I not only found my destiny, but now I have found where I fit in and where I finally belong. My quest to find Quanah Parker has come full circle, and now I need to live life!

Quanah's Training

Quanah did not allow a long honeymoon. Bright and early, he arrived. "We talk," he said. "When I was a young boy, I was resented for being a half-breed among the boys of the camp. I had to fight my way up to overcome that stigma. I had to outdo and out-perform everyone in the camp to find my rightful place. As I grew into manhood, I became a warrior and then leader of the Comanche. When the army came to take us away, I fought. I fought two great wars: the Pease River and the Red River Wars. I clashed with Colonel McKenzie, a good fighter and good leader of the army. But Quanah won! Quanah is still here! I don't want to worry you, but who knows when the drums will speak—trouble! You are now my blood brother, and I wish for you to overcome what I had to overcome. It will be hard, but I see a leader in you! So… here is your Winchester back, and your first assignment is to ride Buck."

I said, "But I have ridden Buck? What's there to learn?"

Quanah said, "No saddle! No bit! Only a bridle with a single rein—bareback or maybe a small blanket. You ride like a Comanche!" So I took my Winchester and scabbard and went to fetch Buck.

With one rein, I was confused. I would signal for Buck to go one way, and he would instead go the right way. Braves laughed! They said, "Horse smart. White man dumb. He goes the wrong way—horse goes the right way!" I let Buck have his head and gave a signal where to go. After all, he was smart—a mustang—and he grew up among the Delawares! It wasn't long before I was back to where I needed to be. I challenged the group to a race! They were eager to go when the flag went down. I was in the back.

96

I gave Buck his head, leaned over and down to his neck, and said, "Take 'em, Buck." I saw Quanah standing on the sidelines. He said nothing, but I think I saw a small smirk on his face. After all that he had endured in his youth, his goal for me was to out-best every brave in the camp. I took a lot of hard knocks and bruises and beatings, but every day I became stronger and more determined! Finally, I prevailed!

At night, I was so happy to get back to my beautiful wife! She was the balm I needed. She would rub me down with loving care and whisper words of encouragement and endearment. In her arms, all pain went away.

As I was finishing up my "required training," I noticed that about half of the braves had rifles and half did not. I didn't ask where they came from! I told the braves I would put on a little show of my ability with the Winchester, which I did, and they were amazed. I said, "If you will share those rifles with each other, I will teach you stance, concentration, and breathing skills while sighting in on your target." So they shared, and I brought them up to speed on the proper handling and firing.

Lastly, I taught all how to break down their weapon and field clean it. Proper lubrication is necessary, but all we had was buffalo grease to improvise. Beating Heart came up with the answer. She produced pure lube from various plants from the forest that nobody knew. Quanah was pleased. Beating Heart was pleased to be part of things, and the braves were on their best behavior when she was present.

Life Goes On

Life went on in camp with the people, and it was a time of good life and living. As time passed, Beating Heart and I would sometimes walk up to the bluff and watch the evening sun go down, taking a moment of solitude for us. We would talk about our future and what might come to be.

Beating Heart became pregnant and, in time, delivered her first baby—a beautiful little girl with black silken hair, a perfect complexion, and the beauty of her mother. I called for Quanah to come and see and name his grandchild. He smiled and took the baby girl in his arms, much like he did with Beating Heart. Then he spoke, "She looks like the beautiful wildflowers of the fields, so we'll call her Little Flower." Then he turned to me and said, "And I will call her father Quantas so everyone will remember the young man who came in search of the great Quanah." He then added with a twinkle in his eye, "Or maybe I should say the young man who came in search of Quanah's beautiful daughter and stole her away!" He chuckled, and life was good. Happiness and love persisted.

When Beating Heart was due again, she had another little girl, beautiful with raven hair and blue eyes. Again, Quanah came to name his granddaughter. He lifted her up in his arms while she was asleep and peaceful. He said, "She sleeps like a baby deer, so we shall call her Little Fawn."

During her third pregnancy, Beating Heart encountered some difficulties, so Quanah summoned the medicine man. He arrived, kept his composure, gently felt Beating Heart, and stroked her hair. He mixed a potion and gave it to her, and she went to rest. There was no drum beating, rattle shaking, or dancing around, and I was relieved—I might have thrown him out otherwise. Without further complications, Beating Heart gave birth to her third child—a beauty like her mother, with raven hair and blue eyes. Quanah was very proud to name this last grandchild. I say "last" because, when I embraced Beating Heart, she whispered, "James, we are complete."

Quanah held the baby to his cheek and said, "She is as soft as the down on a dove. We shall call her Little Dove." As I observed Quanah, a thought struck me—the world does not truly know this man, but they should. He is not merely the "half-breed" some label him as. He is a leader of people—compassionate when compassion is needed, loving when love is required, wise in moments calling for wisdom, and firm when necessary. His desire is simple: to live his life, do what's right for his people, adhere to the tenets of the Great Creator, and get the army off his back.

We and the Girls

Beating Heart and I were so proud and so in love. When we looked at each other, you could see the love in our eyes. We seldom called each other by name but addressed each other with pet names and love names. The old women of the camp just rolled their eyes.

As we grew together, the girls were taught all things that Beating Heart had professed. There was a lot of love from us, but also firmness in teaching the right things to do. And when we gathered together with the people to celebrate various functions, Mom and the girls danced together, and they danced more beautifully than anyone else in camp. They were like the fairies of the wood—so special. You could hear all the *oohs* and *ahhs* as they danced to the drum. The girls were not only dancers; they were well-respected and refined young ladies. I must say, growing up, they had a little tomboy in them because, like their old dad, they bested every boy in camp. Buck was always happiest when the three girls would leap onto his back and head out for an outing. The three girls were very close, and the boys knew to show respect. If you crossed one girl, you had all three to reckon with!

The Poachers

One day, one of our scouts came riding in quickly. He told Quanah that there were a couple of poachers on our land. Quanah said to me, "Mount up! Bring that Winchester and come with me." We went out in search of the trespassers. When we came within sight of them, Quanah pulled up. They turned to face us, and their faces were painted with war paint. Their horses were also painted. They looked as if they were ready for a fight! They turned toward us with weapons at the ready.

Quanah remarked, "Crows! The worst enemy of the Comanche." Quanah continued, "Slowly pull your rifle out of its scabbard. Fire a warning shot over their heads! Do not wound or kill them!"

I pulled out my Winchester, slowly and deliberately, raised it, aimed, and said, "Steady, Buck!" I fired two quick shots at the perpetrators. The shots took the feathers off the back of the two warriors' headbands, never touching the hair on their heads. The two Crows looked at each other in astonishment. They slowly raised their hands in a salute and then turned their horses and rode off. Quanah never looked at me. He kept his eye on them as they left.

Then I heard a low chuckle, and without looking at me, he said, "You, that Winchester, and your horse are one."

When we returned to camp, he said he had something to give to me. He went into the teepee and then came out. He handed me one of those brand-new Colt repeating rifles that the army was starting to use. I didn't question where it came from. I suspected it was confiscated during the Pease River wars. The ammo was the same caliber as the Winchester, so my supply increased. He said, "This is better in your hands than in mine!" I didn't know what to say, so I weakly thanked him. He waited a moment and then spoke, "There is something I need to tell you. The drums of war are faintly telling me that someday in the future the Bluecoats will come for us! When they do, what will your position be? Will you fight against the white men, or will you stay neutral? Or perhaps even join them?"

I answered, "Quanah, there is no life out there for me! I am your blood brother. My family is here—my girls and my wife. If anyone threatens me or my family, I will fight and protect them with my life! No matter who the attackers might be. When that time comes, I will do what I have to do!" He was silent for a moment. I thought I saw a small tear in his eye.

After a moment, he said, "Well said, my son!" So the distant drums were far off, and I hoped that we would never hear them close by.

The Buffalo

Our lives continued in happy times. Our girls grew in beauty and grace. We knew, in time, as the girls grew up, they would marry and not be close by. Even though I was showing my age a bit, I thought Beating Heart was still the most beautiful woman in the world. I couldn't stop telling her that and also how much I loved her. And when the Great Creator blessed me with this woman, he gave me the greatest gift of all. He has blessed us with the great spirit to watch over us. Beating Heart says, "There is a little more to the story. For a long time, I had asked the Great Creator to send me a man I could love and one I could build a good life with. And then you appeared on that fine horse of yours!"

Our reminiscing was interrupted by the scout. "Come quick, Quanah! Buffalo!" There was a large herd of buffalo grazing over the ridge by the camp. Quanah called some braves and me to accompany him. The people needed meat. As we approached and peered over a rise, we saw the herd. We were debating how we could take one down without spooking the herd and causing them to leave the area.

I suggested, "Let me ease down the slope alone, quietly, without disturbing the herd. I can take one down at 200 yards." Quanah crept to the top of the rise to have a look. "There—that big one in the rear!" So Buck and I started moseying down. When the buffalo looked back, I let Buck drop his head and start to graze. Seeing a horse slowly grazing did not seem to disturb them.

When I got within 200 yards, I said, "Steady, Buck," and took down the one Quanah had pointed out. The herd ran a short distance but soon resumed grazing. The braves cut some saplings and fashioned a litter to be pulled by two horses. We descended, field dressed the buffalo, rolled it onto the litter, and headed for camp.

Back in camp, everyone had a role. The meat was butchered; some set aside for that night's celebration. Some meat was smoked for later; the hide was scraped and stretched to dry. As evening approached, the meat was cooked. Everyone gathered for a delightful evening of fellowship. Quanah used these outings and ceremonies to communicate with his people and keep them informed. That night, he raised his hands and gave praise to the Great Creator for the food He provides to sustain His children.

There were many nights that people gathered like this around the fire to eat or celebrate various ceremonies. It was a fun time for all, and we listened to stories from the past to enjoy and learn. Some were true, and some were tales, but tales sometimes make a point! The young men had a chance to tell their stories, and Quanah encouraged the women to speak because he wanted to hear what they had to say. Then old-timers would bring stories from the past, words of wisdom, to carry on tradition and certain tribal trends that need to be passed on to next generation so as not to get lost.

The young braves started in on me to speak my stories of my travels. They wanted to know all about the wagon train, the people, and places I've been. I started with my life in the east, around the Delawares and how they moved out. How they captured Frances Slocum and took her west, much like the Comanche had taken Cynthia Ann Parker, Quanah's mother and brought her west! I told them about how I had purchased Buck from the remaining few Delawares in the area. How the River Man more or less adopted me, taught me how to shoot and train Buck, even totally gifting me with the Winchester. Then when I got to the story about Ajax and Henry the mule, they just laughed and laughed. But when I got to the part about the Lost City and the Natives from Peru, they became very quiet. I did tell them that the city wasn't found but that from whom Ajax had learned to prepare his meat. Also that the natives were descended from Montezuma, the great Aztec ruler, and maybe some of that carried through into Mexico and the Apache nation! I didn't intend to tell so much, but I guess I was on a roll. And anyhow, they enjoyed the entertainment.

Beating Heart and I always enjoyed these get-togethers as much as *powwows* and ceremonial events. As we would sit together and watch and listen, as usual she would be holding my hand or leaning right in or having her arm looped though my arm. We always had to be touching each other somehow. I always hungered for that contact, and I always wanted her smell. Funny how the little things can affect you so much.

Quanah, when a good point was made, would raise his hand and say, "*A'lto!*" (which meant "amen" or "so be it"). I guess it was an honor for the Lakota-Sioux braves who had married into our band. They would say, "*W'ophia thankjka*" (which meant "many thanks") when duly noticed.

Together

When we retired to bed that night, as I held her in my arms, thinking, I started to giggle. I was remembering back to what Quanah said about our first child, "I will call you Quantas, so all will remember you who came to find Quanah...or was it to find his daughter?" She stirred awake and raised her head to look at me. "What are you laughing at?" she said.

I replied, "Oh, nothing. I guess I was thinking about how happy I am." Then I stroked that beautiful raven-black hair across the side of her forehead, and she softly slipped back into slumber. That was us, getting older and still being in love—a love so strong that it would never die. I whispered to her, "I love you, and I always will. I will never leave you!" I guess I realized now that this is where I belong.

When I left the East as a young man, I was on a quest to find Quanah Parker. This is true, but did I realize at the time that I was also searching for something else that was lacking in my life? I was searching for a place where I truly belonged—a place where I could fulfill all my dreams and desires in life, a place where I could find love and be loved! And here was that beautiful woman that I had found on the east side of paradise!

So the journey goes on, and any journey has to start from home. Love's what makes that journey worthwhile. And here it is, and I have found it among these people who were not my people by blood, so to speak, but they became my people through the bond of love. They never saw "white" in Quanah, nor did they see white in me. They looked upon me as their brother. I believed as they believed.

They said the Great Creator had brought them from the earth, and I believed that God had formed man from the dust of the earth, and upon death we would return to the earth—ashes to ashes, dust to dust. They believed that the great spirit would transform their death into a journey that would take them back to the Great Creator. I believed that the Holy Spirit, active in our lives through Christ, would direct us back to God and paradise.

They believed that the great spirit could control all life, even the animal spirits. I believed this, also, because in some cases, an animal will perform an act so strange that it had to come from somewhere. Remember in the Bible how Balaam on the road was stopped by an angel, and his donkey spoke to him three times to warn him of danger—the danger of being struck down by a sword for his disobedience! And Balaam answered his animal three times! So I can respect the beliefs of the people. The true beliefs, that is, for we will find it comes full circle, and we can be in harmony with each other. So with that said, on with the story!

Quanah Troubled and Words
with Beating Heart

Quanah called for me, and I knew that something was deeply troubling him. He spoke, "My son, to you, and only you, I speak. I do not want to trouble the people right now. Very faintly in my heart, I hear drums speak. The time is drawing near, but not now, that the white eye will find us. At that time, we will have to stand and fight. I will have to decide what to do with my people. At that time, you will decide what is best for you and Beating Heart. In the meantime, go on with your life. The time will come when the drums will talk loudly to us."

I said, "Whatever may come, I will be the first to stand with you."

And he said, "I know you will do that, but I will not permit this. What would happen to Beating Heart if you were lost?" So I tucked these words of wisdom back in my memory bank and did what Quanah said, "Go on with life." But I said to myself, yes, but be prepared!

Beating Heart and I went on with life—living and loving. I did not tell her about the conversation! We spent many good times together. We enjoyed all the ceremonies and adventures of the people—the meals together, stories around the fire, the ceremonies and dancing. But mostly, we enjoyed our time together! Our walks to the top of the bluff, looking down on the beautiful valley below and watching the sunset drop through the trees. Sometimes nothing was said, just holding hands and watching. She was so beautiful that I could never take my eyes off her. One night I told her, "I am glad that Quanah had you because you are the most beautiful princess in the world, and I will never leave you."

She smiled that smile that could melt your heart and said, "When you first came here, and when I turned to see you, you scared me! But with you sitting on top of that beautiful horse Buck, I fell immediately in love with you. Right then! I had been praying to the great spirit to send me a beautiful man that I could love, and he, in turn, would love me, would stay with me, and we would build our lives together. And he did! I kept watch, hidden, when they had you tied to that pole! As long as you were safe, I would not disobey my father's intentions, but if there was harm to come to you, I was ready to battle for you! I was amazed when my father called me out and asked if I wanted you! Of course, I wanted you! I wanted you forever! My prayers had been answered!"

Many moons went by in our life of living and loving together. Then one night, I felt Beating Heart slip from my arms. I awoke, and she said, "James! Something is wrong!" That's the night that Beating Heart went down. I called for Quanah; and he, in turn, summoned the medicine man, who then checked Beating Heart all over. He raised his sad eyes to us and shook his head no! He didn't know the sickness or how to treat it.

In the months that followed, I stayed by her side, taking care of her and watching her body slowly shut down. No one could figure out the cause or the cure. The girls were called home. They helped but could only stay so long before they had to return to their people and their own children. With sad eyes, the two old women came to take care of things. I stayed by her side and took care of her needs. She said she loved me, and I loved her. Many moons went by, and one morning, one of the old women whispered to me, "She does not respond! Whisper your love into her ear, she will hear!" I whispered endearments into her ear, and a little later she slipped away. I thought I saw a spirit lift from her body, and her face turned young and radiant! I went to Quanah with tears and a broken heart. The man that never showed emotion had tears falling down his cheeks. He said nothing, he didn't have to! I sat with my princess through the night, weeping. I was a broken man!

This went on for two days, then Quanah came and said, "Beating Heart must go into the earth. The Great Creator waits."

I said, "She will not go in the ground like a dog! I want a crib made for her from fine cedar—scraped to show its beauty, then bound tightly together, and a cover for the crib, also scraped and bound together to fit the top. And I want fine furs upon which she shall rest."

Quanah said, "It is done!"

So my precious princess was laid to rest in a crib made of fine cedar, bound tightly together. A prime buffalo hide covered the bottom. A fine fur of mink was for her to rest her head. All the sides and the bottom surface of the crib's lid was lined with fine furs. The old women had dressed her in her fine dancing clothes. Her people came with fine stones polished from their possessions—turquoise, agate, crystal, and even some rough stones with the Black Hills' gold showing on the surfaces. They laid beautiful wildflowers from the field around her. Then I placed my fine wedding bucks and moccasins, folded neatly, at her feet. Then she was covered with a fine blanket, symbols of the spirit animals woven in, which were woven by the women of the camp. The lid was secured in place and covered with a fine buffalo hide.

Then Quanah offered a short prayer to the Great Creator, and she was put down! Then she was covered. During this time, there were many tears and wailing. Two Comanche braves helped me move a large stone to her head. I asked them if I could have some of their war paint. I wanted blue and red. They also brought white. I painted a field of blue, then a white border around the field of blue, then I painted a large red heart in the field of blue. The people came back when I was finished and again wanted to pay their respects to Beating Heart and respects to me. I received many pats and hugs while the two old women stood by my side! I hugged them, and they left. I stayed there with my love, weeping, and watched the golden sun go down, sad memories flooding my soul! I came back down in the morning.

Alone Again

A few days went by, and Quanah said to me, "I have to wash you up again before you stink!" So here came the two old women again to do the job! They did not laugh this time; they had on their kind faces. They washed me up real good, and then they washed my hair—it was a mess. I had let it grow long, Indian style. They gave it a good washing. After a sun dry, they brushed it out. They made two braids, and as they braided, they worked in a strip of some kind of red cloth. It looked good, felt good, and I liked it. I thanked them for their kindness.

A few moons went by, and my life was a mess, a mess of a broken and lonely man. I could not overcome the grief! I had always said, "The road back from grief is a long journey, sometimes never-ending." Not only the grief, but I felt like somehow my health was slipping with it.

A few moons went by, and the scout came and said to me, "Go! See Quanah! Want talk!" So I went to see Quanah, and his face was drawn.

"The drums have told me! The white eyes are on the move. They come soon. Once again, Mackenzie is leader. He knows too much! I have decided to move my people back west. We go to Palo Duro Canyon. Big place, much hide! There, I make last stand. Do not know outcome!"

I said, "I come with you. You trained me to fight!"

He thought for a while and said, "I would want to take you, but things change. Too dangerous. Beating Heart is gone now, and you are a broken man. Still good, you see, but broken. Now, I don't have to worry about you and Beating Heart. You're a good man, a brother by blood. You are a friend and like a son. My heart would be heavy if I lost you too! I think it's time for you to see animal spirits in the woods. That's the best thing! That makes me happy."

I said, reluctantly, "Okay… I will obey your request, but first, come with me for one moment." Quanah followed me to my teepee. I took the Colt repeater and my Winchester and handed them to him, saying, "These are best found in your hands. Take them with you to Palo Duro Canyon. Protect your people!"

He raised his eyebrows and said, "You don't want to give away your Winchester!"

I said, "Yes, I do. I won't be needing it where I am going! Quanah, I look at it like this: the gun belonged to the old man at the river. He trained me and Buck, and then, with a good heart, he gave me this Winchester. Now, I want you to take it, and I want you to take Buck with you!"

I saw his eyes start to well up, and he said, "I take this with great honor, and I will take good care of your Winchester and your fine horse, Buck!"

Then I said, "I have one more thing to ask. Will the spirit animals talk to me?"

He said, "They will talk to you…if you have a good heart!"

Spirit Land

I did not wait for the people's departure, which was to be soon. I didn't want to have a big to-do about leaving. You know how loners are! So I made plans to pack my bedroll and a few things. I don't know how they found out, but on the morning I was going to quietly slip away, the old ladies showed up with a grin on their faces and a tear in their eyes. They said, "You can't leave before we say goodbye." I didn't know they could talk! They brought me flatbread and jerky to take on my journey. After hugs and goodbyes, they said, "We won't tell!" and I slipped up the trail to the forest above the bluff. I took one more look around before I left—the camp, the grave, and the top of the bluff where Beating Heart and I watched the sunsets together.

I said to her spirit, "I love you." Then I entered the forest. Without direction or purpose, I guess I chose to walk in the upward direction. I figured going up might prevent me from going in circles. I guess that was a different journey because I did not know how, when, or where it would end, nor what I would find at the end (if I even found the end?). It was a long, pleasant walk upward in the forest, and the further I went, the more beautiful it seemed to be.

It was getting near dusk, so I started looking for a place to stop for the night. I had to laugh at myself because I thought it was like a dog looking for a place to lie down. At least I could laugh at myself; that was an improvement. I picked a nice grassy spot near some small pine trees and rolled out my bedroll. I had a little water with me in a gourd but not much. I ate some flatbread and a little jerky and settled in. The stars above were vivid and very beautiful. My thoughts drifted to memories of Beating Heart. I drifted off. My morning was brought awake with a group of cows having a caucus—probably about the intruder sleeping below them! On with my journey for another day.

Several days passed, causing me to lose track. Same routine: keep walking up, find water, eat a bit, curl up in bedroll. Then one morning, I was awakened by the cry of an eagle. Just for fun, I cried back. He started circling around, so I tried my cry again. He came down through the treetops and perched on a sturdy branch outcrop. With care, I moved closer to him. He didn't attempt to fly off, just made his clicking sounds. I said, "I don't have much to offer; just a piece of jerky." I took a piece out of my pack and handed it to him. He took it in his beak, put it under that huge foot of his, and began to eat. I said, "Are you the bringer of what's to come?" He just clicked some more then got quiet. In a few moments, he lifted off and took flight, up, up, and gone. Strange—it made me wonder.

Same pattern of hike for a few days, then I came to a small clearing with a fresh brook trickling beside. It was a good place to stop. As I laid my bedroll down, I saw a movement out of the corner of my eye! Across the brook, on the edge of the woods stood a wolf pack! They looked at me intently. The alpha leader was a beautiful silver-gray, bigger than the rest. She slowly started to move forward, and the pack decided they were going too. Wrong move—she turned on them, snapping and biting, and put them in their place. She watched again, then slowly started her advance! I remembered an old-timer saying to sit on haunches, bow your head, dangle arms between knees, and bow your head. I said to him, "Then what? Pray or kiss my ass goodbye?"

He said, "No. That position is like a wolf, not a member of the pack—sitting in submission. The alpha leader will check it out. If acceptable, the alpha leader will lay its ears back and lick the face of the new wolf; then he is acceptable. If not, too bad! They fight."

"Katie, bar the door!" I said. So I did like the old-timer said: I took stance. The alpha she-wolf padded across the brook and approached me! Slowly, she advanced, sniffing. She came up and got in my face then laid back her ears and frantically licked all over my face. Yes, I'm a wolf! I spoke to her softly, and her ears perked in attention. I said, "All I have to offer you is a little jerky." I slowly retrieved a piece and offered it to her. She took it and put it between her front paws and ate. I cautiously stroked her neck, and she allowed this. When she finished, she turned to the pack.

As she left, I said, "She-wolf," and she looked back! I thought, "Watch my back." She stood for a moment, blinked her eyes, and returned to the pack. They silently disappeared into the edge of the woods. I'm astonished. Is this what Quanah meant when he said, "They will talk if your heart is right?"

The next morning, I leaned in the brook for water and saw a reflection. When I looked up, the she-wolf was at the edge of the woods looking at me, her pack behind. I watched for a moment then said, "Watching my back." A blink of the eye, and then she faded into the woods, disappearing.

Some more travel, and one day I sat down on a log to rest. The bushes moved! Out came the biggest red bear I had ever seen! He sniffed the air, got my scent, then focused his eyes on me. He went up on his hind legs, rolled his head, and snarled, foam dripping from his mouth. He lowered to the ground and beat his great paws in the dirt! Up again on his hind feet, growling. Well, this is it. I've bitten the biscuit! I can't outrun or outclimb this one! Then I remembered another old-timer who shared a story with us about a spirit bear. The story goes, an old medicine man was walking in the woods, gathering his herbs when he was confronted by this rogue bear. As he started to charge, the old man threw up his arms and went into a chant. The bear stopped, and legend goes, the old man and bear became friends and walked together in the woods for many moons. Then they disappeared and were never seen again.

The bear was in his charge, so I leapt up, threw my arms in the air, and yelled at the top of my voice, "Hey ya, ya, ya, hey ya, ya, ya, ya, Spirit bear!" I didn't even know what I was yelling, just something I made up in the spur of the moment! The bear stopped! He looked at me, turned, went a little further, then looked back again. My jaw was jumping up and down like a galloping horse! He looked back again, and I thought to myself, *Does he want me to follow?*

So I did; on up through the woods we went. He came to a honey tree and stopped, put that big paw into the hole, and ripped the tree open. There were bees all over his face, but he kept right at it! The swarm was finally discouraged and left. The bear was eating cones and licking his lips. I wondered if I could have a little of that! So I cautiously reached into the hole and pulled me out a hunk of cone. The bear and I were just looking at each other and licking away! Come dusk, the bear started looking for a place to lay down for the night. When he found a place to his liking, he settled in for the night. I unrolled my bedroll and settled in. Big day!

Pattern Set

In the morning, the bear arose, came around to me, gave me one bump, and started up the trail. In the days to come, the bear was my provider. He would bump me, start up the trail, and look back once to see if I was coming. This went on for days, so many that I lost count. We must have bonded! He found water and delicious berry patches where we ate our fill! He also found edible plants of the forest. One day he broke apart a rotten stump, and the grubs started crawling. He looked at me, and I said, "No! I'm not eating grubs with you." So I still had some jerky left, and that was my meal. I didn't understand what all this was about, but I'd heard stories about the spirit world, and if it was really true, I wanted to experience it if at all possible. I guess I was given the whole show!

As we went along, each day I began to feel some extreme tiredness setting in. I just shook it off. One night, when Bear was settling in, he found some pines with low, hanging branches. It smelled so good! The pine needles had collected below, and it was like a soft bed! Bear crawled in and was soon snoring. I unrolled my bedroll on top of the pine needles and lay down. As usual, my mind went to my Comanche Princess, Beating Heart. I felt a deep loneliness come over me before I drifted off.

The Ascension

Throughout the night, I was awakened with great pain! Then another and another! I was gone. My spirit arose, and I was looking down at the scene like an out-of-body experience. But I wasn't going back into that body; it was dead. I hovered there until dawn started to break. I saw Bear stir and then arise. He came over and gave me a bump. I did not move, so again he gave me a bump. I did not move. He sniffed my body. Then he sadly took his great paw and began to scrape the twigs, pine needles, and fresh-smelling dirt from around me and covered my body. When satisfied that he had a good cover, he took his big paw and patted it down. Then I watched as he lay down and placed his big head on the mound and, for a while, grieved. Then he got up and started up the trail. This time he did not look back. Sad, I thought. I wished that my spirit could communicate with his spirit.

So there I was, suspended, not sure what I was supposed to do. I had heard stories about great chiefs who died and then ascended on a route to go back to the Great Creator. All the tribes built fires on the mountaintops in the belief that it would light their way on the last journey. Well, I certainly wasn't a chief. In fact, I wasn't even Indian. I had just lived with them so long that I thought I was.

So I tried ascending, and it worked. I began to rise and drift above the mountaintops. As I rose, I came into a mist. The mist caused me to lose direction. I became afraid. I called out, "Holy Spirit, I am lost and afraid. I beg you to come to me!" Right away, he was there and took my hand.

"I will lead you on this journey."

I could see nothing. I asked, "Are we going up or are we going down?"

I thought I heard a faint chuckle, and then he spoke, "You are going up, my son. You have been redeemed." Then I saw light within the mist, and I knew that when the mist lifted, the light would reveal all. We came out of the mist into a realm that I could not explain, but it was beautiful beyond description. He could see my puzzlement and said, "This is paradise, and this is where you will be. I must leave you now, but someone will be here to greet you."

As I looked around at all the beauty, I heard a rustle. When I turned, it was Beating Heart! So beautiful, so radiant! She was smiling at me. Tears of joy welled up in my eyes. She moved to me and placed her arms around my neck. I in turn placed my arms around her waist. She said, "James… I have been waiting for you! What took you so long?" And then, she smiled.

I didn't know how to answer, so I said, "Well, I told you that I would never leave you!"

And she replied, "And I told you that I would always love you!" And we embraced. I was home.

Prologue

Near the end of the story, we recall that Quanah had to move his people. In reality, the people were Quadhi, which were a band of the Comanche nation. Quanah was their leader. Yes, he did move into the Palo Duro Canyon to take his last stand. There were many accesses in and out of the canyon. Quanah and his warriors would pop out of an opening and cause many casualties to the army. Consequently, the army did not defeat Quanah or bring him in. The army just kept calling in more reinforcements from other forts, and they even recruited the Texas Rangers. They intended to starve out the whole band since they could not defeat him in battle!

When ammunition and food supplies ran out and people were near starvation, Quanah, who was concerned about the welfare of his people, came out to surrender. His demand was that if he surrendered, he would bring his people out and lead them to the reserve at Fort Sill, which he did. Once there, with the agreement that his people would not flee, they were comparatively left alone.

He taught his people the ways of farming and vocations. He established a church and school. He took back his family name, Parker. Although he was never elevated to chief by the Comanche, the federal government appointed him as chief of the entire Comanche nation, and he became the primary emissary of southwest Americans to the legislature. In civilian life, he gained wealth as a rancher, settling near Cache, Oklahoma. He built a home in Cache, which was called The Star House. He became well-respected by the Whites.

President Theodore Roosevelt often visited him, and they went hunting together (I wonder if he took the Winchester?)

I could fill many more pages with interesting facts about Quanah Parker's achievements, but that would make another book!

About the Author

James Gardner left the east at the age of seventeen to serve his country in the United State Navy. He says, "At eighty-seven, I picked up my pen and began to write. Now at age ninety, I still want to bring you one more story. My stories come from time served in the US Navy and travels with my wife, Anita, now deceased, who encouraged me to write! My stories are a mix with real life and imagination. As I wrote, Cocoa, my faithful Labrador, was always beside my chair. Now my faithful ole dog is also gone. It has brought to mind a quote from the Great Teacher, 'Everything under the sun has a season.' I write and look forward to the twilight."

Other titles by James A. Gardner
Odyssey Down Under
Odyssey Down Under: Parts II and III
Odyssey Down Under: Parts IV and V
Odyssey Down Under: Captain Bligh and Captain Cook

Printed in the USA
CPSIA information can be obtained
at www.ICGtesting.com
LVHW092327210924
791611LV00001B/81

9 798890 614728